Sherlock Holmes

and the

Mystery

of the

Boer Wagon

By

Kieran E. McMullen

Paperback ISBN 978-1-78092-306-2
ePub ISBN 978-1-78092-307-9
PDF ISBN 978-1-78092-308-6
Published in the UK by MX Publishing
335 Princess Park Manor, Royal Drive,
London, N11 3GX
www.mxpublishing.co.uk
Cover design by www.staunch.com

Dedicated

To The Members

of the

Veteran of Foreign Wars

and the

American Legion

Special Thanks To

Christina Johnson

Donna Cacy

Dr. Dan Andriacco

And, as always,

Helen McMullen

CONTENTS

ILLUSTRATIONS

The Cast

Sherlock Holmes	Mr Escott
Dr John Watson	Captain RAMC
Major Drury	Liaison Langman Hospital
Lord Roberts	Commander
Lt Murtry	Junior Aide
Dr Arthur Conan Doyle	Volunteer Surgeon
Major Pelham	Senior Aide
Major Parker	Intelligence Officer
Mycroft Holmes	"The British Government"
Dr O'Callaghan	Senior Surgeon
Dr Scharlieb	Surgeon
Dr Gibbs	Surgeon
Winston Churchill	Reporter
Johnny Moyer	Dresser
Sergeant Weaver	Assistant to Lt Murtry
Frederick Burnham	Scout
Frederick Fredericks	Scout
Clint Cacy	Teamster
Seanan McMullen	Farrier

Keenan McMullen	Farrier
Mrs Foster	Landlady
Fritz Duquesne	Boer Spy
Lt Barthelme	Aide to Lord Roberts

Forward

The adventure I relate here came to me in a most unexpected manner. I had thought that I had seen the last of my days of active campaigning with the forces of the crown when I was invalided out of Afghanistan during the Second Afghan War as I described in *Watson's Afghan Adventure*. This assumption on my part proved to be a particular error, for twice more I would be called back to the flag; as I relate here in the Boer War and again during the Great War. (See *Sherlock Holmes and the Irish Rebels*.)

This was a dramatic time in the history of the empire. The old century was about to close and a new one open. A new century of discontent that would see revolution and attempted revolution across the globe. Not only were there the Boers to deal with but the Boxers in China. The Matebele had only recently been quieted after the Zulu. In the first 18 years of the new century there would be revolution in Russia, China, Indo-China, Mexico and a "War to End All Wars". It was both a terrible and fascinating time.

This story is about both a success and a failure. Holmes was indeed at his best, but like the problems that related to the round-up of the Moriarty's forces there would be issues that would plague Holmes through no fault of his own. His was work to be well proud of. I can honestly say that but for his great effort the war in South Africa might not have gone as well as it did, at least, to the taking of Pretoria. The remainder of the war and the work of Lord Kitchener are for another time.

John H. Watson

Captain, RAMC

Sherlock Holmes

and the

Mystery

of the

Boer Wagon

By

Kieran McMullen

Chapter 1

AN INVITATION

It was the winter before I was to turn forty eight years of age and eight years since the death of my second wife, Mary. I was once again sharing lodgings at Baker Street with my friend, Sherlock Holmes, and spent more of my days writing than practicing medicine.

I had found that my scribblings about Holmes and his unique faculties left me with both time and money to pursue other interests (and the racing season was not far off). It was a good life. I enjoyed the writing and Holmes, though he fussed about my turning a "serious study" in criminalistics into penny dreadfuls or schilling shockers, was conscious that my writings brought him new cases and allowed me a living.

It was Saturday, the third of February 1900. It was a rather cold and dreary afternoon. My friend Thurston and I had been playing billiards for the better part of it at his club. Thurston was a nationally known champion. Why he should play with me I have never understood, for rare was the occasion when I beat him. None the less, we were good friends and an afternoon at sport was well spent.

It was during our third game that I noticed my literary agent, Dr Conan Doyle, enter the room. He, like I, had been a trained surgeon who found more fulfilment in writing than in medicine. I had gone into medicine largely due to the circumstances of my stepmother's death in Australia.[1] Why Doyle had entered medicine I was not sure, though I suspected a similar tragedy of some kind in his own family. It was not the type of question one asked.

"Ah, there you are, Watson," said the big man, extending his hand. Doyle was hard to overlook in a crowd. He was tall, athletic, had a great moustache and a booming voice. He drew attention by his mere presence.

"Doyle," I replied, taking his hand, "what brings you here? I don't owe you the final on the blackmail case until next week, do I?"

Doyle chuckled and shook his sizable head. "No, Doctor, I was wondering if I might impose on your time tonight? I'm meeting with a few friends about this dreadful war we are in."

Suddenly remembering Thurston's presence, I introduced the two men.

"Thurston?" said the big man. "Champion billiard player and table maker? Indeed this is a privilege, sir."

---

[1] See Watson's Afghan Adventure

"No more than mine, Doctor. I am delighted to meet you. I greatly enjoyed 'The White Company', marvellous novel."

Though Doyle tried to hide it, his delight at the praise was evident.

"You have a brother-in-law named Hornung, don't you?" continued Thurston.

Doyle nodded.

"I thought so. He's trying to make a run at Watson's clientele with his new stories about Raffles, the Gentleman Thief. Don't say as I get the concept, but the story is good enough."

"I'll be sure to tell Willie you like his work."

Doyle turned back to me as Thurston started circling the table for his next shot. Stories were fine, but billiards was serious business.

"So may I count on your presence tonight, Watson?"

"I suppose," I replied, "but can't you say what it is all about?"

"Time enough for that. Until tonight then, say about eight. We'll be meeting in a private dining room at the Cecil Hotel. Now, if you gentlemen will excuse me, I

have some other important business I must take care of."
With a nod Doyle turned and was gone.

"Well, your friend Dr Doyle is a bit mysterious," sighed Thurston.

I picked up the chalk and wandered to his side of the table.

"I cannot imagine what all that is about unless he's made a committee to raise funds for the soldiers or something."

"You'll find out tonight. Now if you don't mind, it's your turn, so hurry up and miss so I can run the table." I laughed and for the moment forgot about Doyle and his mysterious invitation – long enough to lose two more games to Thurston.

It was later that evening as I was preparing to meet Doyle that Holmes interrupted my thoughts. "You're right of course, Watson; they always say it will be a short war."

"Holmes, how did…. Ah, never mind. You won't trick me again."

I picked up my hat and gloves as I made for the door to our sitting room.

"I was looking at the picture of Gordon, then at the photograph of my reunion with the 5th and finally at the calendar. Simplicity itself! The government always says it will be a short little war, and it never is. Am I right?"

"Watson," said Holmes putting down his paper and rising, "you have it exactly." I was grinning like a Cheshire Cat as Holmes went to charge his pipe from the Persian Slipper.

"So will you go to South Africa with Doyle?"

"What? Nobody has said anything about going to fight the Boers. Doyle would be the biggest target on the battlefield. No, here you're wrong Holmes. I'm sure this dinner will be about some committee to get pledges. Though I admit with the Northumberland Fusilier (my old regiment) going, I have an urge myself."

"Good old Watson. You'd do well by them too." Holmes lighted his pipe. "Have it your own way. I'll tell Mrs Hudson you'll be back in a year or two."

With that Holmes seated himself by the fire and picking up the paper proceeded to fill the air with clouds of smoke.

"Really, Holmes," I muttered as I closed the door behind me.

Chapter 2

AT THE CECIL HOTEL

The Cecil Hotel is only a few blocks from Charing Cross Station. It occupies about three and a half acres of land along the Thames and fronts on the Strand. It is a wonderful hotel. At the time it had been newly rebuilt and was reported to be the largest hotel in the world. The main restaurant of the hotel faces the Thames and the gardens. The orchestra sits on a raised platform across from an enormous fireplace. Everywhere one looks there is polished marble and granite, tapestries and fine American walnut.

Passing the billiard room with its four full sized tables, I regretted that Doyle hadn't extended his invitation to Thurston. I was to meet with Doyle in a small dining room off the main restaurant. Even here all was elegance. At one end of the room stood an open balcony looking out on the river.

"Right on time, Doctor," bellowed Doyle from across the room. "Come meet your fellow invitees."

Crossing the room, I found myself in the company of four other gentlemen besides Doyle. "We are all here, old boy, to convince you to join us on a great adventure and to serve your fellow man."

"I hope I do that already. At least I try," I responded. I was already getting an uneasy feeling that Holmes was right. Just what type of committee was this?

"Let me present my fellow adventurers," Doyle continued. "Mr Archie Langman, Dr O'Callaghan, Dr Gibbs and Dr Scharlieb. Gentlemen, this is my friend Dr John Watson, formerly of the 5th Northumberland Fusiliers and a man I hope you will help me convince to come along on our great adventure."

Hands were shaken all around and smiles passed. I was offered a whisky on a tray by a sour-looking waiter and considered taking two. "Just what is it that you gentlemen look for me to do?" I asked, taking a sip from my glass.

"Oh," replied Doyle, "plenty of time for that after dinner, but first gentlemen, let us repast!"

Dinner was filled with small talk of local events. Cricket occupied most of Doyle's conversation. Though an enthusiast, my knowledge of the sport and its folk heroes was miniscule in comparison. Gibbs and Scharlieb were both young and enthusiastic about their profession as surgeons so for a while talk drifted into medicine. O'Callaghan, it appeared was a gynaecologist with an extensive practice. If O'Callaghan is involved, I thought, this surely can have nothing to do with going to war as Holmes believed. My confusion was growing.

At last our seven courses were done and I was hoping to retire to the billiard room. Instead, brandy and cigars were passed, the door to the kitchen closed, and the one to the balcony opened. "Shall we bring our colleague on board?" smiled Doyle, looking around at the faces at the table.

"By all means," replied O'Callaghan.

Doyle leaned forward, elbows on the table and looked straight at me. "It's this way, John. We need you to come with us to South Africa as a member of the Langman Volunteer Hospital."

He leaned back and looked around the table as heads nodded. "You see," he continued with glass in hand, "the army has need of doctors and hospital equipment. You are surely already familiar with the sorry state of our medical corps. Oh, don't protest, the army already admits it.

8

"Archie's' father, John," he pointed to Langman, "is footing the bill for a 50-man hospital with all necessary equipment to go assist as soon as we can get men and supplies put together. Archie will be Chief Administrator of the hospital. He has been given a Lieutenants Commission in the Yeomanry.

"Dr O'Callaghan is Chief of surgery, and Drs Gibbs and Scharlieb his assistants. I, myself, am going as an extra surgeon. We'd like you to come."

"I'm honoured, gentlemen," I replied, "as you can imagine. But I must be honest. My skills, I'm sure, do not compare with Dr Gibbs or Dr Scharlieb here. Why, I spend most of my time writing these days."

"John, John, don't deprecate yourself. We know you are a skilful surgeon, plus," Doyle looked about for nods of re-enforcement, "we have another motive in asking you."

I leaned toward Doyle as he put both palms on the table cloth. "Yes?"

"It's like this," injected O'Callaghan. "We need your military experience. For two reasons really…."

"Quite," interrupted Doyle. "John, we have a problem. We've been required by the War Office to have a military liaison officer with us."

"And you want me? But I've been out of uniform for the past, oh, almost twenty years."

Doyle held up his big hand. "No John, you don't understand. The problem is that they have given us a liaison officer."

"What?"

"Unfortunately, they've given us a Major Drury, an Irishman. Oh, he's pleasant enough, but a bit of a martinet when he's crossed. Let me just say he has the failings of his race.

"Don't look at me like that, O'Callaghan; you know that Drury drinks too much. Why Drury has even told me that the height of his ambition is to leave the service and to 'marry a rich widow with a cough'.

"I'm afraid he does not like to be crossed and, John, we need you, your ability to handle people, your knowledge of military matters and surgical skill. Will you help us?"

I must say, it was rather an awkward moment for me. Fine professional men were asking for my help in a noble cause. Was I up to the task? "So you need me to be the liaison to the liaison is that the idea?"

"You might say that a large part of your duties will be to keep us on the straight and narrow and on good terms with the army," responded Gibbs.

I sat back and thought for a moment, all eyes looking at me. "Well, I've no big practice to keep me here, but I do have a task master for a literary agent. Someone will have to do something about him. I'll never get that blackmail story done in time."

Doyle almost leaped over the table to shake my hand, crushing it in his large paw. "Watson! Watson! Stout fellow, I knew we could count on you!"

"When do we leave?" I asked. "I still have much to do."

"We leave by the end of the month, old boy, but for tonight, billiards and brandy, eh?"

Doyle and I retired to the billiards room, but the others made their excuses and departed.

"What compelled you to take this journey on?" I queried as I circled the table looking for a shot.

"Actually, my mother," replied the big man.

"Your mother? Why if I know her, she would be dead set against you going."

"Exactly!" Doyle missed another shot. "You see, she and I have very opposing ideas about this war with the Boers." He leaned heavily on his stick. "The Boers have refused to give the franchise to Englishmen just because they were late in coming to the interior. Outrageous! And they started the shooting you know."

I was half listening as I looked for a shot.

"Mother believes that it is all about gold. She believes that Cecil Rhodes is to blame and that the Boers are in the right. Why, she even claims that the Cape Colony Minister, Milner, has caused the war." I was now paying attention. "To quote her 'we are doing to the Boers what Rome did to Britain' and 'Gold is the root of the matter'. Well, we are past any discussion of that now."

"We are in it good now, I'll admit," I said. The Boers are not to be trifled with. They are not savages against Enfield rifles and Maxim machineguns. 'Black Week', as the papers call it, was a considerable set back. Four major defeats for British forces in a week shows that we are in for a fight."

"And," sputtered Doyle in reply, "the Boers are taking in French, Italian, German, and American volunteers. What kind of countries let their citizens fight for a foreign government?"

"Yes, well, I'm afraid it is getting late." I put down my stick and took Doyle's hand. "It will be an adventure, I can see that. I'll be in touch tomorrow." With that, I started for the door.

"And oh," I remarked over my shoulder, "that Milverton Story - after the war!" Smiling, I waved and left.

Chapter 3

A CALL FROM MYCROFT

As I walked up the stairs at Baker Street, the hall clock was just chiming midnight. I had much to think about. Physically I had no question as to my abilities and I felt myself an adequate surgeon. My ability to mediate between a civilian hospital and an army Major, that might not be as easy as it first sounded.

"Watson, turn around and try for a cab. We have an appointment with Mycroft."

"Holmes, at this hour? Whatever for?"

"It seems, Watson, that the crown is in need of our services. I told the messenger to inform Mycroft that we would be available whenever you returned. Come, man, or you'll get no sleep at all tonight and you know how you get!"

Holmes rushed by me on the staircase and was out the door. I had to fairly run to keep up. He continued his blistering pace for the better part of three blocks before we found a hansom at such a late hour.

The horse was moving almost before I was in the seat as Holmes gave the driver instructions for the Diogenes Club. The Diogenes Club, of which Sherlock's brother Mycroft was a founder, was a gentlemen's club for the "most un-clubbable men in London". It was a club where no member was allowed to take notice of any other member and talking was allowed only in the "Strangers Room", where non-members might be brought on rare occasions.

"Now, Holmes, really, what is this all about?" I stammered.

"There is no sense in speculating before we arrive and are given information. Here is Mycroft's note."

Taking the paper, I read Mycroft's almost indecipherable scribble: "Sherlock, come. Bring Watson. Mycroft."

"It surely does not tell one anything, does it?"

"No, but it is an affair of state which would require one to go somewhere, I'm sure. So that eliminates Mycroft."

I spent the next few minutes trying to come to a conclusion on what the note could possibly mean, but such an exercise was completely meaningless.

Few were the lights in the windows when we arrived at the Diogenes Club. The club was the third leg of a triangle that encompassed Mycroft Holmes's world. His government office and his flat were the other two legs of his stool. It seemed like such a small world, and yet Sherlock's older brother moved entire pieces of a global empire from that little triangle. Mycroft had proven before that, as Sherlock claimed, at times, he WAS the British government. Before we reached the door of the club it was opened by a commissionaire who stood silently as we entered. Without a word, he closed the door and started down the hall to the 'Stranger's Room'. It was here that we met Mycroft.

"Ah, thank you Fritz," said Mycroft rising from the Queen Anne chair by the fire. "You may go now. There will be no need for your services for the rest of the night."

Fritz did not reply, but clicking his heels and giving a Prussian bow, withdrew, closing the door behind him. "New man, Franco-Prussian war veteran, wounded left arm," stated Holmes.

"Yes, we took him on about a month ago. His English is horrid, but that doesn't matter so much here," replied Mycroft.

"Good of you to come and bring the doctor. Whiskey and syphon are on the table if you like. I, for one, am going to return to the fire." Mycroft seated himself while I made busy making whisky and sodas for myself and Holmes. Sherlock dropped into the chair across from Mycroft.

"Tell me, good brother, why have you dragged two middle aged men out in the dead of night? What great state secret has been purloined?"

Mycroft looked more exasperated than riled by Holmes's remark.

"In a way you are correct of course Sherlock, but it's not so much state secret as secrets, plural. There is also a question of materials gone missing. These are things I need you to look into for me at some great distance from here. With the current state of affairs I dare not leave London myself."

"Nor would you," smirked Holmes.

"Well, alright, nor would I." Mycroft rose from his chair as I handed Holmes his whiskey.

"In case you are unaware, I know affairs of nations don't interest you, just crime in the streets, we are at war in South Africa with the Boer Republics: the Orange Free State and the Transvaal, or South African Republic as they like to call themselves."

"I've heard something of it, yes." My, how Holmes liked to bait his brother!

"Well, you may not know that things are also about to explode in China as well."

"Now that, I was unaware of."

"The short version of that is that I expect the lid to blow off over there any time now. A group called the Boxers or Righteous First is about to try and throw the major powers out of China by revolution and they have the secret backing of the Chinese government. They will not succeed, of course but when it happens, it won't be pretty."

"Well, if you know about the plot, you can stop it, surely," I imposed.

"Doctor, if there is one thing you should have learned by now, it is that governments never act to avert a crisis until it is upon them. Besides the Chinese, the Boers are in touch with the Irish Republican Brotherhood trying to make trouble there. And some woman with the preposterous name of Maud Gonne is trying to plot the blowing up of British troop ships with dynamite made to look like coal."

"Surely not, nothing so heinous!"

"Oh yes, Doctor. And a volunteer unit of Irish and Irish-Americans captured our cannons at Colenso. Some former American Colonel, an Indian fighter named Blake and an Irishman named MacBride are leading them under a green flag."

Mycroft turned back to Holmes. "But China and Ireland are not why I asked you here, Sherlock. I just mention it so you understand that our resources are stretched and I have more that South Africa to worry about."

"Mycroft, would it not be best to sit down and come to the point?"

Mycroft gave that same exasperated look and re-seated himself.

"Sherlock, someone is passing our war plans in South Africa to the Boers and I need you to find that person."

"Good, Lord," I exclaimed. "How can such a thing happen?"

"Oh, the usual, Doctor. Money, promise of reward or fame, or perhaps a threat of some sort, you know, to one's reputation or physical harm to a loved one. There are a million variations.

"But surely Milner would be on top of such a situation!"

Mycroft looked disgusted.

"Milner is the fool who got us in this mess. He and Rhodes! They and their gold and Cairo-to-Cape Town railroad."

"But I thought this was about the treatment of Englishmen in the Boer Republics."

"Doctor, do you think Jameson's raid a few years ago to try and overthrow the Boer Republics was about the franchise? Of course not. Rhodes paid Jameson to try and start a revolution because the largest deposits of gold and diamonds lie in the Boer territory between the Cape Colony and Rhodesia."

"So Doyle's mother was right." I murmured, sitting beside Holmes.

"If she said that, she is a very insightful woman. But to get on with this," he sighed. "Things have not gone as well as they should. Early on we sent ten thousand soldiers to Natal. This action precipitated the war. I know the Boers attacked first, but I can't say I blame them.

"The Boers are well armed. Over the years they have bought modern Mauser rifles and French cannon. Every Burgher is trained to shoot and ride, and they can live off the land."

Mycroft pulled out a map, and spreading it on the table, started to point out places I had only heard of.

"Our forces are invested at Ladysmith, Kimberly, and Mafeking. We greatly underestimated the Boer's fighting ability. Methuen and Buller are good generals, but they've been fought almost to a standstill by an amateur army. Lord Roberts has been sent to save the situation but what is really going to save it is a massive influx of troops. Not only do we have to fight an enemy in front, the distances are so great that we have to leave thousands of soldiers to protect the railroads behind our advance."

"So, brother," chimed in Holmes, "you still haven't stated your need for us."

"Sherlock, someone is providing our troop movements on the ground to the Boers. They know our next move before we make it. I need you to go to Cape Town and wherever else you need to, to find and stop this leak of information.

"You will be going as a correspondent of the Times of London named Escott. One of your favourite aliases, I believe. The doctor will go as a medical correspondent. His knowledge of military matters should help immensely. Your reason for being there is allegedly to report on all the war material that has gone missing from the docks. And the doctor is looking into the failure of the Army Medical Corps."

"I'm afraid I can't, Mycroft. Just tonight I gave my word that I would go to South Africa with Mr Langman's Hospital," I responded.

"That is very inconvenient," said Mycroft. "Can't you get out of it?"

"Heavens no," I blustered. "I gave my word."

"Bother!"

"That may work out just as well," declared Holmes. "Mycroft, can you see to it that this Langman's Hospital is sent forward to wherever Lord Robert's headquarters will be?"

"Easiest thing in the world."

"Good, then I will have Watson where the information may be being passed. What say you, Watson? Up for a two-sided game?"

"Of course, Holmes, whatever I can do."

"Good, then that is settled.

"Mycroft, I will want full particulars tomorrow. In the meantime, I will start my investigation here. Is it possible that known information here is going by a circuitous route to the Boers?"

"Oh that is possible surely. Portuguese East Africa is a hot bed of spies and supplies for the Boers. The rail line runs from the Port of Laurenco Marques in Delagoa Bay straight to Pretoria. In fact, there are hotels there that cater to the spies of the world."

"Secrets passed that way, though, would be more strategic than tactical. The Boers know the timing and that means a leak in South Africa."

"Good night, then, Mycroft." said Holmes standing. "Come Watson, we need to get you your rest. You have much to do."

Chapter 4

ON TO CAPE COLONY

The next three weeks were busy, to say the least. I saw little of Holmes, since when I was not with Doyle interviewing men to support the hospital, Holmes was down at the docks and warehouses looking into how, where, and when supplies or information might be moved.

It was near the end of our third week of preparation that I finally ran into Holmes in our rooms.

"News of the war goes well, Holmes," I said, putting up my stick and hat.

"It is truly a wonder, Watson, truly a wonder."

Holmes was clipping the end off of one of his cigars.

"I assure you, Watson, there is almost no reason to have a secret service if you are a power opposed to England."

"Whatever are you talking about?"

"Just read the newspapers, my dear fellow. That's all one need to do, just read the newspapers." Holmes threw the *Times* on the table. "Every ship we send out to the Cape Colony is listed In the *Times* and every other paper. Not just the ship, but the unit going, the number of men, and the officers by name.

"It tells one when they leave, where they are going, and when they have arrived. Why, with the telegraph it takes less than twenty-four hours to know they've disembarked and only a fool would not know their route depending on where they land; Cape Town, East London, wherever.

"Defeats, victories, unit strength, all reported openly in the press."

"Yes," I replied, "in a way it is disconcerting."

"There's much more going on than Mycroft would have us believe."

"How is that?"

"Watson, I already know there have been a number of plots to blow up the docks in Cape Town. The Cape

Boers are not all friendly and there is one by name of Duquesne, a Fritz Duquesne who appears to be the ring leader of the sabotage plots. I've also found out that there are more than supplies missing - in fact, the missing supplies are minimal. What is missing is gold. About 260,000 ounces of gold so far. Quite a considerable sum."

"My God, Holmes! That is a king's ransom!"

"Quite a bit more than that, Watson." Holmes shrugged and started for his favourite chair. He sat and was quiet for a moment. "But tell me, how go your plans with the hospital?"

"Well enough. Major Drury isn't as bad as Doyle seems to think. He just has a more rigid attitude about things. I'll be able to handle him.

"Other than that, we are about ready. We have all fifty men and our equipment. We sail on the 28th on the P & O ship the Oriental. Poor Doyle is having fits though."

"Too long delayed, eh!"

"Yes, he's convinced it will all be over and done before we get there. I try to assure him that wars are never short, but with Kimberly relieved, he's quite positive he'll miss everything."

"Men can be such fools," declared Holmes and picked up his paper."

"You do know that Doyle will have to be brought in on your masquerade, don't you?" I inquired. "After all he knows you."

"Yes, hopefully he can be quiet about the matter."

"Once I tell him it's a matter of national importance, he will be quiet as the sphinx. He'll be thrilled to be 'playing a part', as it were."

"Quite. I should thank your friend Paget, too."

"Why is that Holmes?"

"Ever since he drew my likeness in that silly hat, no one recognizes me without it."

Holmes chortled at his own joke and picked up his paper.

"Now Holmes, you can't tell me there is so much gold missing and drop it there!"

"Nothing to tell you. Milner says it's accounted for, but my sources say it went missing on the way to Cape Town and is in the Orange Free state. Mycroft agrees that Milner is hiding the loss." With that he put his nose back in the paper. "Oh, one more thing Watson. I will be sailing with you on the 28th, so be good enough to go ahead and talk to Doyle."

On the 27th of February, I found myself, along with Doyle and the rest, watching the loading of our equipment on the *Oriental*. I had already spoken to the "Big Man" about "playing the game" - when he met Mr Escott of the *Times*. He was excited that he was to be involved and assured me he would not open the bag.

The following morning, we found ourselves loading aboard our last-minute provisions and ourselves. I admit I was excited to be off. Thoughts of my time in Afghanistan, things I hadn't thought of for years, came rushing back. Mycroft had arranged that I should hold the rank of Captain in the RAMC, allowing me to deal more easily with Major Drury, for which I was grateful.

We were quite a conglomeration on our little ship: Officers of Engineers, Light Infantry, Borderers, Yeomanry and Quartermasters, men of the Royal Engineers, Warwickshire Regt and the Essex regiment along with five surgeons, five dressers, and forty men of the Langman Hospital.

Our first stop was to be Queenstown for five hundred officers and men of the Royal Scots and our first incident.

Holmes had joined us in the early hours and was introduced all around as an outbound correspondent. He was well met and hit it off immediately with Major Drury. It was probably the early sharing of a whisky flask that brought the two together. I felt that my best course was to stay away from Holmes as much as possible lest I give away his disguise.

Another traveller on our ship was a man by the name of Conway. He was a munitions merchant who had been known to sell to the Boer Republics before the war. He was treated with courtesy, but not much more by everyone except Holmes and Drury. The three would play American poker well into the nights with Holmes constantly winning and then forgiving Drury's debt. Only Conway would be the loser.

The trip overall was of no great consequence. We had no foul weather and only a few incidents come to mind. The first though set a disquieting tone upon us. As the lighters ferried soldiers and equipment to the ship at Queenstown, an Irishwoman aboard one of the craft threw a white towel on board and shouted out, "You may be after finding it useful." Before anyone could respond, the lighter pulled away. I would learn more of what lay under the surface in Ireland years later.[2]

The rest of our three-week journey brings only a few memories. Doyle organized a cricket match in Cape de Verdes. He also gave a lecture on the war to all hands one night. The toughest part was the illness brought on by the Enteric Fever inoculations. Unfortunately, the inoculations were not mandatory and the illness brought on by it caused men to refuse to take it. This would have

---

[2] See Sherlock Holmes and the Irish Rebels, MX Publishing, 2011

devastating consequences, for we would lose more men to disease than to bullets in South Africa.

Holmes, Conway and Drury were fast friends before we were half done with our cruise. Though Doyle knew Holmes was not really a correspondent for the *Times*, he insisted on explaining to him at length, his theory of having 20,000 soldiers stand shoulder to shoulder, and by pointing their rifles in the air at the fixed elevation, bringing a rain of bullets onto the opposite side of a hill. It seems that neither the *Times* nor the War Office were interested in his theories.

On the night before we reached Cape Town, Holmes asked me to visit him on the fantail. He would be getting off the *Oriental* and going to start his investigation in earnest. I was now feeling a bit guilty about abandoning my old friend.

"Perhaps I should stay here with you, Holmes. After all Langman, is an excellent administrator and Drury will get the hospital forward. You may need me here."

"No, Watson. I need you up near the headquarters with Roberts. If it is as I believe, the gold has every possibility of being in Bloemfontein. We'll get war news here. Unless I'm much mistaken, Roberts will have pressed forward by now. Mycroft will see to it that the hospital is where I need you to be."

"But why would the gold be in Bloemfontein?"

"No gold has been shipped to England since the start of the war, Watson. Milner says that the last gold shipment out before the war is safely in hand." Holmes paused to light another cigar. "However, if that is true, why hasn't it been shipped? Neither the mine owners nor the government have been given a good answer." He looked out into the night as the glow of his cigar lit his face.

"You remember the armoured train that Cronje destroyed?"

I nodded.

"I believe Milner lost the gold that day and is hoping to regain it before he is discredited. Keep your ears open, Watson. A shipment that large cannot have gone unnoticed. Someone in the army knows something. And keep on good terms with Drury. If he learns anything everyone will know it, I assure you. He is most congenial and talkative, especially after a few whiskeys."

"What about this fellow Conway, Holmes? Has he anything to do with the missing supplies?"

"Oh, easy enough, Watson. I've known for quite some time what he is doing. He delivers goods here to the dock in Cape Town. The supplies are signed for and then a few Boer stevedores re-mark the boxes as something else and send them on to Portuguese East Africa."

"The cads!"

"Yes, I'll hand Conway over to Milner tomorrow and we'll put an end to that. But what I want are his confederates on the dock. Someone must know Duquesne and about the plot against our facilities. If I can solve that and find the gold, we'll have done good service. There is still the question of information to the Boers. It could be that the information is passed here, but more likely it will be forward."

"I've no doubt of that, but what shall I do while I'm waiting for you to contact me?"

"Listen and watch, Watson. Look for unusual relationships or people who appear to have problems which distract them from their duties. Someone in need of funds or who seems to hold a grudge of some sort."

Late the next afternoon, we arrived at Cape Town. By evening Doyle, Langman, Drury and I had gone ashore to get information, while Holmes was off to the Times office to report in and would collect his box on the morrow.

The news at Cape Town was both good and bad. The good was that not only had Kimberly been relieved, but so had Ladysmith,. Cronje had surrendered, and Bloemfontein, the capitol of the Orange Free State, had fallen to Lord Roberts. The bad news was that we were to stay in Cape Town until a final determination was made about the use of the hospital. I had to smile to myself, for I had no doubt Mycroft would win out.

On the 26th of March, we would leave Cape Town for East London on the East coast to unload and make our way to Bloemfontein.

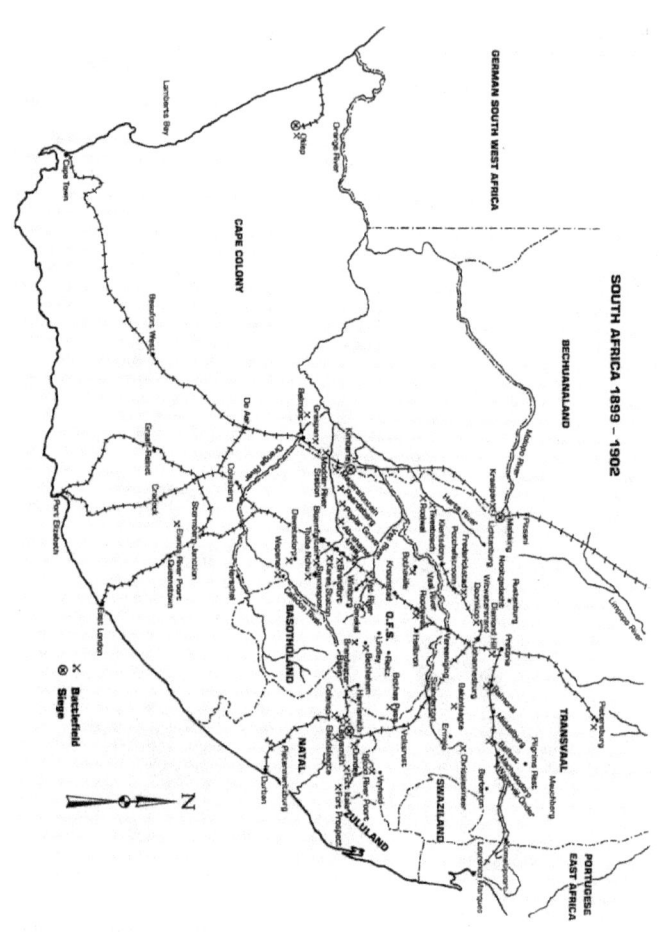

Chapter 5

BY RAIL TO BLOEMFONTEIN

Before our departure from Cape Town, Holmes came to the Mount Nelson Hotel, where Doyle and I had put up until news should come of our assignment. Doyle was fascinated by the conglomeration of wounded officers, ne'er-do-wells, adventurers, and adventuresses to be found in a capital at war. To me it seemed much as I remembered Bombay and Watson's Hotel in the early '80's. Human character had not changed. I suspect that adventuresses were present with the armies of Alexander the Great as much as they were with the Army of General Hooker in the American Civil War and would always be with us.

As Doyle had gone off to view the imprisoned Boers where they were held at the cities race track, I met Holmes alone on the veranda of the hotel.

"About ready to leave, Watson?"

"Yes, Holmes, we're off to East London with the tide. Hopefully we'll be in Bloemfontein in a few days."

"Oh, you will be Watson. But here comes the man I really came here to see."

Coming up the walk was a gentleman who appeared to be in his mid-thirties. He was quite tall and angular and dressed as a professional man. Tripping along next to him was a boy that I would venture was about eight years old. The boy held tightly to his father's hand with his own left. In his right he held a wooden sword with which he occasionally parried the assaults of an imaginary foe.

"Excuse me," said Holmes, stepping toward the pair. The gentleman stopped. "I believe you are Mr Rathbone, are you not?"

"Mr Escott is it?" replied the man. He released his grip on the boy and the two men shook hands.

"Yes, I'm glad you could come. Let me present my friend, Dr Watson. He is recently arrived like me. Who might this young soldier be with you?"

"This is Basil. Say 'good day' to the gentlemen, Basil."

The boy stood straight as an arrow, and saluted with his wooden sword in the best military manner. He smiled from ear to ear when I returned the salute. "Good morning, sirs."

"Shall we have a seat?" Holmes indicated some chairs on the far side out of the sun.

"I'm afraid I had to bring Basil along. His mother has the other children and is packing for our return to England tonight." He looked down at the boy and sighed. "I'm afraid this one spends all his time fencing and playing with a magnifying glass that he has taken from my office in Johannesburg. I'm sure I don't know what is to become of him."

"He is a fine lad," I said. "I suspect he will do well."

The boy smiled at me again and moved over closer to his father. When we had seated ourselves Holmes looked about a moment and, seeing we were quite alone, continued.

"Watson, Mr Rathbone was, until recently, a mining engineer in Johannesburg and one of brother Mycroft's best men." Holmes turned back to our visitor. "Can you give us any word on the gold shipment?"

"I thank you for the kind words, sir. But, truth be told, it was touch and go getting out of the Transvaal. The old boys are pretty smart up there. They suspected I was not just a mining engineer but they had no solid proof. It was suggested that it was time for me to go somewhere else by some men I knew well. I couldn't risk things with the family as I would have alone." He looked at his son and patted the boy's shoulder.

"As to the gold," he went on. "There is no doubt it left Johannesburg. My sources here assure me that it never made it here to Cape Town or to Durban or East London or Port Elizabeth or anywhere. I am convinced the Boers have it. I also think that Lord Roberts has moved so swiftly that it may have been overtaken and it has been hidden. That, sir, is all I know."

Rathbone rose from his chair, as did Holmes and I. We made our farewells and Rathbone and little Basil departed. Basil had to present his sword salute. I very solemnly returned it. The last I saw of the boy he was fencing his way down the street vanquishing who knows what enemy.

"Well there is confirmation, Watson. Milner is lying through his teeth. When you get to Bloemfontein I want you to contact a Lieutenant Murtry of the Dragoon Guard. He is a junior aide to Lord Roberts. He will be your contact with me. I believe I can clear up this business at the docks fairly quickly. Conway has given me all I need about the supply shipments. My problem is Duquesne. He has not showed among those we have rounded up so far. I don't believe he is here. I think he has acted through intermediaries everywhere. We don't even have his description."

"But surely," I replied, "he had to talk to someone. Someone has seen him."

"Oh, they have Watson, they have." We walked out onto the lawn.

"The trouble is," continued Holmes, "that none of the descriptions match. He's tall, he's medium height; he's stout, he's slim; he's got brown hair, his hair is blond; he has a Boer accent, he sounds like an American." Holmes sighed.

"He's been quite elusive and done very well at presenting himself not only in different disguises, but in different guises - as lumberman, banker, and gentry. I look forward to meeting the gentleman." We walked toward the veranda steps.

"Remember, Murtry will know me as Escott and will pass information between us."

"I'll remember, Holmes." We shook hands and Holmes started to leave.

"One last thing, Watson. There is a young man up there named Churchill. Keep away from him if you can. He's attached himself to a colonial unit and is acting as an independent correspondent."

"Lord Churchill's son? Glad you warned me. He's got quite the reputation for getting in and out of scrapes. Already escaped a Boer P. O. W. camp hasn't he?"

"Yes and caused all sorts of problems inside and outside the government. Just keep clear. We don't need to advertise our presence."

We bade each other farewell and good hunting. I watched Holmes disappear into the crowd on the street.

Later that day, the *Oriental* started the short journey to East London, where we arrived two days later on the 28th of March.

Our landing went well; men, equipment, supplies of every kind were quickly off-loaded onto the docks. But here was all the chaos of an army in motion. Trains came and went all times of the day and night carrying food, clothing, ammunition, men, horses, cannon and wagons. Somehow a fifty man volunteer hospital was to be found a place on one of these trains.

Here I must give praise to Major Drury who was able to make us a priority for space and to the transport officer, Leo Trevor, whom Doyle apparently knew from amateur theatricals. We were given a choice of moving in two trains or waiting a week to go together. We pressed forward. Doyle appeared to be everywhere, lending both his mind and his physical abilities in loading the hospital.

Though the distance was merely about three hundred and fifty miles, the trip would take days as we travelled through the beauty of the Veldt and the stench of dead flesh. Dr O'Callaghan approached me in the twilight of our first day out as we sat at a siding. (All the senior members of the staff had chosen the first train out, leaving the dressers to come on with the second part of our equipment.)

"Whatever is that stench, Dr Watson? It's been going on for miles."

"Death, Dr O'Callaghan."

"Death?"

"Yes, it's the hundreds of unburied horses, mules, and oxen that an army uses up in a campaign. Even as we speak, there are men in Australia, Canada, and the States buying up tens of thousands of replacement animals."

O'Callaghan looked out the window into the gathering darkness. Doyle approached and sat next to him.

"But, Watson, surely the animals are taken care of."

41

I had to laugh a bit inside. How little these gentlemen knew about where they were going.

"Yes, yes of course." I responded searching my pockets for my pipe. "You must remember, Doctor, that most supplies and equipment move by animal power. The men depend on them to keep them alive, to bring them food, water, and ammunitions, to move them about so they can chase the Boer who are well horsed.

"But every time you move a horse, he also needs food, water and sleep. So now you have more horses, moving supplies for the first horses. And if the first horses moving through an area have grazed it off, what do the second horses eat?" Having found my pipe, I charged and lit it.

"I see, and there are casualties of course." continued O'Callaghan.

"Certainly. Which is the bigger target, the horse or the man? Bring down the horse, you bring down the man. If you want to capture your enemies' artillery or supplies, how can you best do that? Kill the horses in the traces, of course."

O'Callaghan looked shocked.

"Doctor," I went on, "without the animals the artillery can't escape. Then all you have to do is kill or capture the men."

The two doctors looked back out the window.

"That smell, Doctor is war. You might as well get used to it or light a pipe."

I got up and leaned out the window. The train lurched into motion as a southbound ambled past and once again we were on the main track. The camp-fires of the thousands of men left to guard the supply lines glowed in the darkness as we slowly rumbled past. It seemed like every few minutes we stopped to let other trains depart south. At Sturmberg we waited half a day as repairs were being made on the temporary bridge ahead that crossed the Orange River.

It was while we were stopped at Sturmberg that I received my first communication from Holmes. It was a telegram that simply read, BEWARE THE TWO HEADS STOP ESCOTT.

"What the devil does that mean?" I thought. Two heads? Two heads of what? Holmes was infuriating. Somehow I was just supposed to know the meaning. I would file that information away in my mental "lumber room" and ponder on it.

Once we crossed the Orange River, the sites of war were more evident - farms without livestock, burned off pasture, and fresh graves could be seen along the railway.

We did not reach Bloemfontein until five o'clock in the morning on the second of April.

Chapter 6

TWO GOOD MEN

The Scots, who had been with us and occupied most of the space, were off the train, formed up and marching away from the rail yard almost before the train had stopped.

As Langman and Drury started to organize the offloading and consolidation of our equipment, I went in search of information. No one seemed to know where the second train with the rest of the hospital equipment was, so I left the rail yard in search of Lord Roberts' headquarters.

"Where the devil has Doyle gone?" shouted Drury, as I went bye.

"I'm sure I don't know," replied Langman.

"I'm off to the headquarters," I called. "I'll see if I can find him." And without looking back waved my hand and headed for town. It was not fifteen minutes later when who should pass me but Doyle, well mounted on a borrowed horse, with two other men riding along.

"Off to see the Boers, Watson. Supposed to be some shooting up ahead. Get a horse and come along."

"No, I have things that must come first." I replied. "And keep your head down," I shouted as he and his two new friends charged off to the North.

Lord Roberts' headquarters was in a large hotel in the middle of town and easily found.

Getting to see Lieutenant Murtry was also fairly easy. Clerks are much easier to get along with when a subordinate is asked for rather than the Commander. The clerks always assume you are, like them, a cog in the wheel, with business and not there to make a problem for them or others.

Murtry greeted me in a small anti-chamber off the side of Lord Roberts' offices. "Welcome Dr Watson. Mr Escott told me of your coming and asked me to look out for you. May I show you where the hospital is to go? Wonderful cricket pavilion really. Come this way."

We walked back out of the hotel. As we started down the street, Murtry leaned close.

"Things are not all peaches and cream here, Doctor. I've been instructed to help you by a message from White Hall and told not to inform my superiors. Puts me in a bit of a bad spot, you know.

"Mr Escott has me looking for evidence of any unusual shipments out of Bloemfontein, anything really unusual or particularly heavy. But that doesn't really tell me anything. It would help if I knew what he really wanted."

"He is a frustrating man, I admit," I whispered. I thought for a moment of how often Holmes had kept me in the dark and how much more valuable I felt I could have been if he had informed me what the problem was. I made a decision.

"Lieutenant, we are looking for two things. First, we are looking for a large shipment of gold that has gone missing. Second, we are looking for a man named Duquesne. We think he is running a band of spies and smugglers and is responsible for the missing gold." I decided not to mention that we knew plans had gone missing.

"Alright, sir. Is there a description of the man?"

"No, unfortunately, there is not."

Murtry frowned as we walked a distance in silence. The sun was almost half to the top of the sky as we approached the cricket field.

"You know sir, with all the freight coming and going every day, it would be almost impossible to open every crate to search for gold. Do you know if it's in bars or coin?"

"Bars, at least it was. It could be in any form by now."

"Yes, here's the area for your hospital, sir. You'll have to make arrangements at the rail yard for transport of your equipment up here. As soon as we get back to the hotel, I'll give you a note to the coordinator that Lord Roberts considers you priority."

It was a good two hours before I returned to the rail yard. By then Doyle had also returned, having found that a soldier must get use to alarms and that no battle was in the offing. It was only a short time later that the second half of our equipment was located. We were soon moving up the hill and to the cricket pavilion in a combination of local and army transport wagons.

"Expecting lots of wounded, are you?" The remark came from a large-boned Irishman atop a Boer wagon pulled by four mules. His brown slouch hat had the brim turned up in front with a green cockade. He hadn't had a shave in about a week and his dark blue waistcoat and trousers were patched in a number of places. His boots showed a new sole on one and a hole in the bottom of the other. He smiled down from the driver's box, a pipe in one side of his mouth. I liked him already.

"It's like this, my friend; best to have what we hope we don't need."

"Aye, I'm for that sure."

"Have you been in Africa long?" I asked. It might be good to have a friend among the teamsters. Especially one who knew the area.

"Six years and some." he replied

"Gold fields?" I asked with a grin.

"Sure, it seemed a good idea at the time, your excellency. It's just Rhodes and his kind already had it all. So here I make my fortune, me and my four ladies." He flicked the reins and called, "Step up, Victoria, pull your share now, step up."

"What's your name?"

"Cacy, sir. Step up, Victoria! Walk on, now. Walk on." The wheels of the wagon groaned under the weight of the boxes.

The wagon was a small freighter with Archibald wheels and a canvas cover across the bows. On the canvas was painted a yellow harp about a foot and a half high. The box and wheels had been painted not long ago.

"You take good care of your wagon." I ventured.

"Only way to make me living, sir. Best keep it in order. You're making me tired now, ya are. Get up on the box, sir; we've still a bit to the cricket field."

Cacy pulled up while I climbed on and we sat in silence the rest of the way.

Doyle, the first back, was busy directing the arrangement of beds and equipment. Langman, Drury, and I soon decided to keep out of the way of our Scottish friend and let him arrange whatever he wanted. He was an unstoppable force. By nightfall tents were up next to the pavilion and enough room was available for about fifty patients. I dreaded the thought of so many, but it was best to be ready. That night we showered for the first time in days and went to sleep under the stars on cots we had placed on the roof of the pavilion. We were ready for patients, but my thoughts were not there.

I was watching the moon as it moved slowly across the sky and wondered where Holmes was, and what had he meant by his curt telegram, "two heads"? What the devil was he talking about? I pondered this until I drifted off to sleep.

Chapter 7

WATER

As the sun rose and the Army started to stir, I wandered over to the edge of the roof putting together the first pipe of the day. Below I could see my new friend Cacy and his four mules moving slowly down the street toward the edge of town. He saw me and waved a hand. Snapping the reins, he called out "Victoria, step up I say, step up." Victoria leaned into the collar for a moment and the mules started into a trot. Victoria would get the rest going then back off herself. Smart mule.

"Hello, Doctor Watson." It was one of the dressers.

"Good morning, Moyer. Beautiful day, is it not?"

"No sir, it's not. We've no water. Have you seen Major Drury?"

"No water? Ah, no, Major Drury is staying in town. It seems one of the senior aides, a Major Pelham is a friend and he has put up with him. Not sure where. Let me get Doyle, you look for Mr Langman. We'll get this solved." But we were not to 'get it solved'.

Having awakened Doyle and informed him of the situation, we went below and started checking pipes. There appeared to be no breaks nor any sabotage. Moyer came back to tell us that the water was off everywhere. Clean water was critical, so Doyle and I decided to go to Army Headquarters to find out what we could. Here we found Drury in conference with both Major Pelham and Lieutenant Murtry.

"Ah, Doctors, glad you're here. I'm afraid we have bad news." Pelham had been the first to notice us and speak. Pelham was a fairly small man, not taller than five-foot-four, I would say. He had brown hair, brown eyes and a moustache that drooped just below the corners of his mouth. His grin seemed somehow artificial, but I noticed that the droop of the moustache was used to try and cover a scar on his left side that extended from the corner of his lip. It was perhaps a sabre or lance wound that had been not well treated and in healing had caused this facial distortion.

Murtry greeted us with a smile and a "good morning", while Major Drury sat shaking his head and muttering at a map.

"Where the devil is the water?" burst out Doyle. It was a remark not like him at all.

"Doctor," replied Pelham, taken a bit back by the outburst, "we are well aware of the problem, but you see, this is a war and our enemy will use all at his disposal to defeat us.

"You may not be aware that just a few days ago, we lost control of the waterworks which supplies Bloemfontein."

"It is here," he continued while pointing at a spot on the map. "It is about twenty miles East out by the mountains. Broadwood had a devil of a time trying to get back. He lost a considerable force and a number of cannon at Sanna's Post, a river ford between here and there."

"Makes sense they would cut off the water," said Drury. "I wonder why they didn't burn the town before they left."

Everyone looked at the map for a moment.

"Where does all this leave us, Major Pelham?" I asked. "Is there to be a relief force to retake the works?"

"No, not right now. There are wells about the town and these will be reopened. That should suffice for now. There won't be any excess of water, but we should have enough."

"When was the last time any of these wells were tested or treated?" Doyle was already beside himself.

"I have no idea, Doctor, but the engineers are working with the few city workers left in town to get some pumps up and running. Most of the units will have to rely on the water wagons. Major Drury will keep you informed. Now, if you'll excuse me, I will need to get back to my other duties." Pelham had obviously dismissed us.

Drury, Doyle and I left for the hospital as Murtry and Pelham went back to their papers.

"This could be catastrophic," commented Doyle, taking the outside steps three at a time. "Has Pelham no sense of what this may mean?"

"No," I replied, "he does not. And doesn't much care either. He has no concept of what is going to happen. His army may be wiped out by disease, but he doesn't see disease as his concern. Battles are his problem, sickness ours."

The rest of the day was spent trying to assemble a system by which water could be treated before we used it. Doyle gave strict orders that water was not to be used unless boiled first. We took all the precautions we could, yet we knew only too well what was coming.

Later that evening, I went in search of Lieutenant Murtry. He was to be found at his desk, but upon my arrival, he recommended we take a walk to the stables so he could check on his horse.

He said nothing as we walked, but once beside his horse, a bay gelding of about 15 and a half hands named Boy-O, he began to update me.

"No patients yet, Doctor?"

"No, not yet. We should be getting some wounded in tomorrow, but for now all is quiet." I paused a moment, looking about. Only the stable guard was present and he was out by the corrals. "Any word from your men?"

"No, sir, it's hard when they don't really know what they are looking for. And as far as unusual activity, well, what is unusual in a war? I've a couple of sergeants who are watching to see if more supplies move to any unit than should reasonably be needed, and we're keeping an eye on the locals, but I honestly don't know what else to do."

"Nor do I," I admitted.

Murtry picked up a brush and idly rubbed Boy-o's back.

"It hasn't been a good day, Doctor. Besides the water being cut off, we've word that two companies of the

Northumberland and three of the Royal Irish have surrendered at Redderburg. Lord Roberts is not happy."

"No, I imagine not. Any word on a force to retake the water works?"

"Sorry, Doctor. Lord Roberts won't move until he thinks the men are rested and ready. Can't afford another loss like Sanna's Post. Bad for morale and bad in the papers. Not that he really cares about the papers, but when he leaves here he wants a straight push to Pretoria. He wants to end this thing."

"Sad about his son being killed in Natal."

"Yes. He doesn't show it much, but we can tell it has really saddened him. Well, sir," Murtry threw the brush in a grooming box, "I've got to get back, got to brief our new chief scout about a job for tonight."

"Why a new chief scouts? Where is the old one?"

"Burnham? Been missing since Sanna's Post." We started walking back toward the hotel. "Don't know if he was killed or captured. American chap. He did exceptional service in the Matabele Wars. In fact, I understand he was in Alaska when Lord Roberts sent for him to come here and help. Came as fast as the ships would bring him. Best scout and tracker in Africa. Good fellow too, for an American."

"Who's the new man?"

"Named Frederick Fredericks. How is that for lack of imagination? He's a Cape Boer, but trustworthy, I suppose. Seems to know the area, speaks Dutch and a few native dialects. Hope he measures up. Anything else, Doctor? I must get back."

"Yes, one other thing. Does the phrase 'the two heads' mean anything to you?"

Murtry thought for a moment. "No, can't say as it does. Only thing it brings to mind is drama. You know, the two faces, comedy and tragedy."

"Hum, yes. Well thank you, Lieutenant. Be sure to let me know if anything comes up."

I started my walk back to the hospital lost in thought. As I walked around the back of the hotel, I nearly walked into the side of a wagon.

"Easy there, your Lordship, you'll dent your helmet."

It was Cacy, looking down from the wagon box.

"Ah, Mr Cacy. Sorry I was lost in thought. What are you doing here?"

"Back from my rounds, sir."

"Rounds?"

"Aye, I go each morning and make the rounds of local farms and get what I can fresh for the hotel and the boarding houses. Farmers are afraid to come in. They're afraid they'll be arrested or shot for just living here."

"Rediculous!"

"Not to them, sir."

"Aren't you afraid of the Boers?"

"Not at all, at all. I carry no gun so each side knows I'm not fighting. And I'd as soon sell to Boers or Brits. That is, if they have gold."

"Seems to be a chance you're taking," I replied. "Must be off, wagon's a bit dirty isn't it?"

"Aye, clean her up tonight. Take care, Doctor."

I continued back to the hospital to report what little I had found out. I was consideralby disheartened by the news of two compaines of my old regiment having surrendered. Not finding any sign of gold or the man Duguesne just compounded my ill mood.

As I passed the boarding house where Pelham and Drury stayed, I noticed Drury through the window in apparent deep conversation with Mrs Foster the landlady. She was a widow of about forty, and while I had not noticed a cough, she at least had assets of two kinds so perhaps she would meet the major's requirements.

On arriving at the hospital, I relayed my news about the lack of a force to retake the water works. Doyle spent the rest of the night blustering about the incompetence of the military. Something he would never say to Roberts himself.

In my absence, we had received about five cases from one of the other hospitals. None were severe, but it had buoyed the men up to now actually have something to do that they felt was worthwhile.

The rest of the night passed uneventfully.

Chapter 8

THE SCOUTS

The next two mornings passed as the first. As dawn came up, I smoked my first pipe and watched Mr Cacy and his four mules come past on the way to their rounds. I had added an A-frame tent to the roof so that I might avoid the coming rains and remain at the pavilion if needed. Doyle was searching accommodations in town.

By now we had about twenty patients who were split up among the five of us. But in all truth, the dressers and orderlies had things well in hand at this point. A week later this would not be true.

This morning I was the first doctor to appear in the ward. I was met by a small flurry of activity. A man in somewhat rough clothing was being attended to by Moyer. He gave every appearance of being a Boer, but by his accent, he was obviously an American. He was about the height of Major Pelham, but with bronzed skin and grey-blue eyes. He was exceedingly muscular and seemed uninjured. He wore a moustache, but no beard.

"Doctor Watson," called Moyer, looking up at me. "Sir, I'd like you to meet Captain Burnham. He just escaped from the Boers."

"Captain, I've heard about you," I said extending my hand. "They were afraid you might have been killed."

"Just captured. Bad bit of luck. But I'm here now." He took my extended hand in a vice like grip.

"What seems to be the problem?" I asked.

"Nothing," replied Moyer. "But Major Pelham sent him down here to get checked out. He's been traveling alone on the Veldt about five days since his escape. Just needs some rest and good food, I'd say."

I turned to Burnham. "And what do you say, Captain?"

"I say it's time to find a place to sleep, a good horse, and get back to work." His smile filled the room.

"Then that is what the doctor prescribes," I grinned. We shook hands again and he left with a nod to Moyer.

"Well," said Moyer, replacing his instruments. "I shall remember this."

"Why?"

"You don't really know who that is, do you?"

"Burnham, an American and Chief of Scouts."

"Yes, sir, used to be a scout for the American Army. He fought Apaches and Cheyenne, scouted for us in the first Matabele War, and fought with Baden-Powell in the second Matabele War. They say he ended the war single-handed when he killed their medicine man M'Limo. He has also been put in charge of training the long range sharpshooters. Quite the fellow."

Moyer finished putting his things up. "They also say he never says a word about any of his life. Just goes about his business."

This was a man Holmes and I could use. If there were unusual movements, this is the man who would know it.

I finished my minimal rounds and decided to find Major Drury. He had not been seen for the last two days. Though he really wasn't needed, his appearance here and there might help with assuring a constant flow of supplies. After trying the boarding-house, I went to army headquarters, where he was also absent. However, to my surprise, Lieutenant Murtry was anxious to talk to me.

"Oh, Dr Watson. I may have some good news for you this afternoon. Close the door, will you? Right."

Murtry came from behind his desk as I shut the office door.

"I've a sergeant named Weaver," he continued in a hushed conspiratorial tone. "He has noticed something odd. There are boxes of canned goods missing. Not a lot, but a few. The problem is that none of the units have noticed any shortages in their requisitions. The food seems to be getting where it's supposed to be, but the count is off at the depot." He looked at the door again.

"Interesting. But if the units are getting the goods, where is the problem? Is it a simple miscount, is it being sold on the black market out of the depot, or perhaps the unit cooks are trading it off for local food or favours?" I pondered out loud.

"Could mean nothing, of course, Doctor. But you said to watch for the odd event and that is what we've found so far." Murtry walked back around his desk as a knock came at the door.

"Enter. Yes, Fredericks, come in won't you? Let me introduce you to Dr Watson. He's assigned to Langman's Hospital down at the cricket pavilion. Dr Watson, Frederick Fredericks. He's a scout that Lord Roberts has just put on to assist. What can I do for you Fredericks?"

Fredericks was a young man. He stood about five-foot-ten and was in his early twenties by my guess. He was clean shaven with short brown hair and brown eyes. He was in shirt sleeves and breeches with high riding boots. His slouch hat was pinned on one side in the Boer manner and pushed to the back of his head. He was an impressive figure with a giant smile.

"Glad to meet you, Doctor. Lieutenant, Major Parker would like to talk to you. He said to bring your file on someone called the 'Black Panther'."

"I'll be leaving you, then," I said getting up to go. Murtry was pulling open drawers looking for his file. "I suppose Fredericks that you'll be staying on even though Captain Burnham is back."

"Yes, Doctor. Seems Lord Roberts wants me to concentrate on finding this 'Black Panther' fellow. Burnham is pretty lucky you know."

"Why is that?" I asked.

"Boers must not have known who they had. They have put a price on his head dead or alive. They'd have watched him closer if they'd known."

"Alright, Fredericks, tell the Major I'll be there in a minute, will you? Hold on, Doctor, I've one more thing for you." Murtry had evidently found his file.

"Right, see you later, Doctor."

When Fredericks had closed the door, Murtry came back around the desk. "See, Doctor, this is part of what puts me in a bad position."

"What does?"

"The 'Black Panther', of course."

"I'm afraid I don't understand."

"Duquesne is the 'Black Panther'. Now I'm caught between two parties, both looking for the same man and I'm not supposed to tell either what the other is doing."

I admit I was somewhat at a loss to help the young man. "Lieutenant, do what you believe is in the best interest of the command." I started through the door my hand on the door knob. "I do not envy your position."

By noon I was back at the hospital and, to my surprise, so was Major Drury. He and Archie Langman were deep in conversation over the number of cots and linen required at the hospital.

"You were supposed to come here fully equipped, sir, and not require extra materials from the army. Sustenance and replacement of equipment as needed." It was Drury and he seemed in a foul mood.

"We did not come prepared for so many, Major. We came prepared to hold fifty patients, but Dr O'Callaghan and Dr Doyle say the men we took in this morning is only the start of the problem. In a week our numbers will double and we'll need more tents, cots, linen and men to help. We must be prepared!"

Langman looked away from Drury and saw me.

"Captain Watson! Perhaps you can make the Major here understand that with all the extra cases we need help from the Army Medical Corps."

"Afraid I've come in in the middle of the conversation Archie. What's going on?"

"We've thirty beds of our fifty filled now with wounded and regular sick call, and we just added five with enteric fever. Dr Doyle and Dr O'Callaghan say that it is just the start because of the water being cut off and we need to double our size for what's to come." He turned back to Drury, glaring at him. "And we need the army to help!"

"Enteric already?" I walked over to Drury. "Major, if the water works are not retaken we'll be losing men in the hundreds, if not thousands to fever. Mr Langman is not exaggerating. You are a doctor, you've seen it before."

Drury stared at me a moment and I could almost see him thinking. "Alright, Dr Watson, you're right, we've been through this kind of thing before. Not like these civilians." He slid his eyes toward Langman. "I'll get with the depot and get all I can. Mr Langman, give me a list and one man to help in case I need a runner. Good day gentlemen."

"Thank you, Doctor," said Langman as we watched the Major depart. "He's a bit hard to deal with these days. Spends his time either with that Mrs Foster or drinking with Major Pelham and that's fine, but right now we have use of him."

I excused myself and went to the ward. If we were about to start a bout with enteric fever, this is where I needed to be. I had made it a special interest of mine since it had caused the death of my step-mother. Now I would put that knowledge to use far beyond what I had ever imagined.

Chapter 9

MURTRY HAS AN IDEA

Within three days, the ward was full to over-flowing and men were dying at an appalling rate. All the hospitals were beyond capacity and we, who had planned for fifty had three times that number. Men would soon be dying at the rate of fifty a day. If Roberts didn't move his army, he would have no army, and yet he still made no move to take the water works.

On the 10th of April, Doyle was invited to dine with Lord Roberts. I considered myself fortunate to not be included in the invitation, for I was afraid of what my frank friend might do or say to Lord Roberts. The retaking of the water works was most prominent in his mind.

I had now developed something of a routine. Every morning I would wave to friend Cacy from the roof, work the day in the wards, and at night meet Lieutenant

Murtry by the stable so he could brush his horse and we could share what little information there was.

It was the night that Doyle was dining with Lord Roberts that a number of curious things occurred. I had made my usual visit to the stables. Murtry had little to impart. Each day Sergeant Weaver had reported four or five cases of canned goods missing, but had not been able to find the culprit. I had now come to regard this as a petty theft issue, but I did not want to dampen Murtry's enthusiasm, so I let him continue to speak of it. Fredericks had been out among the Boers trying to identify the location of the 'Black Panther', so far, to no avail. Burnham had been on a number of scouts and provided some good information on the placement of some of the Boer commandos. Among them was the Irish Brigade under the American, Blake.

"Seems Colonel Blake rides a horse he calls DG," mentioned Murtry. "Captured it from the Dragoon Guard. His Brigade is armed with Krags and some Lee-Metfords that they took at Dundee."

"I'm sorry, Doctor. We don't seem to be making much progress. We know that every time we move a troop or company, they move to counter it. But the question is, is it because they see us or because they are told? I just don't know."

"What does Major Parker say?"

"Our Intelligence Chief?"

Murtry thought a moment.

"I think he believes there is a leak inside the headquarters, but for now he is checking up on the lower echelons - you know, clerks, telegraphers, people like that - who have to be used to transfer orders."

Murtry brushed Boy-O for a few minutes in silence. "I've got a theory, Doctor, but I need to check it out."

"What is the theory?"

"No, I might be accusing an innocent man and I wouldn't want to do that."

"Come, come, it's just we two. Surely you can tell me."

"No, doctor. I'll let you know tomorrow or maybe the next day if it proves out!"

"Suit yourself, but keeping things secret is unwise," I sighed. "I'll see you tomorrow."

"Good night, Doctor."

"Good night, Lieutenant. And don't take any chances."

"I will." He grinned.

I started my walk back toward the hospital lost in thought when I heard laughter coming from a barn to my right. It was actually the barn behind and belonging to Mrs Foster's boarding house. The laughter was easy to recognize. I knew it was Cacy before he walked out of the barn. With him were two other men. All seemed to be in the best of spirits and that is what I attributed it to.

Seeing me, the laughter stopped abruptly, but Cacy's head leaned over as if to squint through the coming darkness. Recognizing me, he laughed again and waved.

"Evening, Doctor. How are you this fine evening?"

"Well, Mr Cacy and you?"

"Fine, fine, sir. My mates and I have finished for the day and are about to go to the Yager's Hotel where a man may get a drink. Will you joint us?

"I appreciate the offer, but I must get back to the hospital. Perhaps another time."

"Suit yourself, doctor."

"Been shoeing mules tonight?" I asked.

Cacy stopped abruptly. He was like a crow as his head twitched side to side. "Why do you ask, Doctor?"

"I could see the glow of a forge inside the barn." I replied. He looked back at the barn and when he turned back, he was his jovial self. "Ah, sure. Me and Seanan and Keenan here were shoeing their horses."

"So you are a man of many skills."

"More than people know," he said putting a finger to the side of his nose. "More than people know. Good night, Doctor." With that, he and his two companions turned on down the road.

I did not know what was to be made of his odd actions, but I had more important things to do. I had a ward of patients to look after.

Chapter 10

ENTERIC

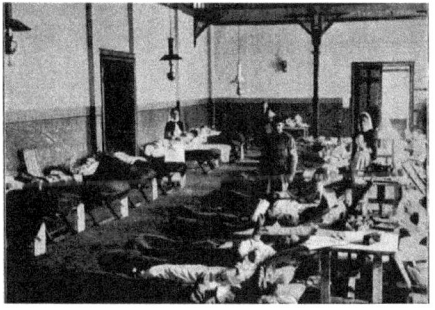

Conditions in the hospital were worse the next day. All fifty beds were filled and more were on the floor. Drury, to his credit, had done what he could. That morning, as I watched Cacy drive his team up the road, a detail of soldiers were erecting additional tents and offloading supplies to augment our hospital.

Doyle had come back from the night before in a better mood with Lord Roberts' assurance that the water works would be re-taken 'as soon as practical'."

I smiled up my sleeve at Doyle's announcement. He did not understand the secret code of the military. What Lord Roberts was telling him was that he would move when he was damn good and ready. Sometimes one has to learn slowly and the hard way.

Lord Roberts had agreed to visit the hospital on Doyle's insistence. That afternoon, true to his word, Roberts appeared.

The effect of the visit was greater on the men than on Roberts. They were impressed that the Commander-in-Chief should take time to visit them and morale was much bolstered.

Murtry and Parker had accompanied Lord Roberts, but it was Doyle who made all the introductions.

On being introduced to Lord Roberts, I saluted and then shook his proffered hand.

"I want to thank you, Lord Roberts, for having saved my life in Afghanistan," I said.

"I?" he puzzled.

"Yes, sir. I was among the wounded at Kandahar. Your relief force saved us."

"Ah, Kandahar. Great march that. Gave them a good thrashing! We'll do the same here, sir. We'll have it over soon!"

"Not if we don't get fresh water," interjected Doyle.

Roberts looked daggers at Doyle. "I've told you, Doctor, as soon as we can. Now, I must be back to headquarters. Major Parker, the horses. We've got to meet some reporter for the *Times*, Mr Langman or I'd be glad to stay a while. Always busy, you know." With a further sideways look at Doyle, he left the pavilion with Parker and Drury bringing up the rear trying to smooth things over.

Murtry pulled on my sleeve as the others left the room. "I was going to let you know about Escott. He arrived about four this morning. He said to tell you he would be on an official tour of the hospital this afternoon."

"Does Lord Roberts know his true identity?"

"No, I don't believe so. He refers to him as 'another damned reporter', but he's received word from the war office to talk to him. I'll try to let you know what else I find out."

"How comes your theory?" I asked. "Any new thoughts?"

"I'll tell you this much, sir. I think I'm getting closer. It involves canned goods, Sarvins, and two kinds of potato diggers." He grinned.

"What?" I exclaimed.

Murtry didn't wait to explain, but hurried off to join Lord Roberts' party, as we could hear the horses departing.

"And two kinds of potato diggers? Whatever does he mean?" I muttered out loud.

"Whatever are you talking about?" Came a voice.

"Nothing, just talking to myself."

Doyle had re-entered the pavilion.

"Looks like we're to be extra shorthanded now that the real work has started. O'Callaghan has decided to go home. He leaves tomorrow. He isn't one for roughing it, I suppose. We'll at least give him credit for trying."

"He couldn't have picked a worse time to leave. We're already over full. How many more cots have we?"

"We'll be able to hold a hundred by tonight. Best make rounds now."

The rest of the day was the real start of the horror for us at the hospital.

Enteric fever, or typhoid as it should properly be called, is a disease for which, as I write this, there is no cure other than time, a strong constitution and good care. Perhaps in the future science will solve this problem. We know it's cause - unsanitary conditions and contaminated water.

Within a week, our hospital was overflowing. One hundred and sixty men were on the cots and on the ground.

The fever runs a course that lasts about four weeks if one is to survive, less if not. It starts with headaches, thirst, lethargy, and aching in the limbs. Many is the man who believes he's just "not feeling well". Then comes the coughing, spitting, thick tongue and fever.

The fever increases each day until it peaks and stays at 104 degrees for a number of days. Along with this will be a rapid pulse of 110 or more. By the end of the second week, the disease is usually at its' worst. There is diarrhoea; bloating and the muscles have uncontrollable shaking. By the end of the fourth week the patient should be getting better. That is, if he is to recover.

I had been fortunate in Afghanistan and survived my bout with enteric fever. As I said, one of the keys is good care. For in many cases, the lower intestines will tear and once blood is seen, there is not much hope. Men must be kept quiet and not allowed to move about. Everything must be constantly disinfected, or not only will the patients die, so will the staff. For the diarrhoea we would give five to ten drops of aromatic sulphuric acid in water. If men were allowed out of bed, they would surely tear their thin intestines. All we could do was use hot water bottles to keep in body heat and give a pint of normal salt solution under the skin. At no time could we give the men any form of solid food. The best things were tea, coffee, boiled rice water, and best of all, milk. We tried to get fresh milk, but that seemed impossible and condensed milk had to be shipped all the way from England. All we could do was our best with what we had. By the end of the week, the hospitals would be losing fifty men a day. In all we would lose thousands to fever. More men than would be lost than to any Boer Commando.

Chapter 11

TWO HEADS

Holmes came to the hospital late in the afternoon that day. He had been invited to dine that night with Lord Roberts and had little time to spend with me.

Having greeted him as Escott, I took him on a quick tour of the hospital. Doyle played, or should I say over-played, his part, welcoming Holmes as Escott in a voice loud enough for the world to hear.

When we were able to get back outside, I started to fill Holmes in about all that had happened. He listened attentively until I had finished then took his pipe from his pocket and I did the same. We sat upon one of the benches outside the pavilion. Neither of us spoke for some time as we filled our pipes and puffed slowly.

"All you have told me is very interesting, Watson. I must spend some time pondering on it."

"But you, Holmes, what has happened? You've said nothing. And what the devil did your telegram mean, 'Beware the Two Heads' or some such nonsense?"

"No nonsense, old boy. You've not run across the two heads or you'd know what I had referred to." Holmes leaned back and puffed. "As to the first part of your question, I can say that it is done for now. Duquesne's minions, like Moriarty's were easily gathered. The head man eluded us, however. In fact, I believe he was gone about the time that we arrived. The ports are safe for the moment. I'm also convinced that while Cape Town is filled with spies, thieves and charlatans, the loss of information is from up here, not down there."

"And the gold?"

"No sign of it. Milner has been, shall we say, less than candid and forthcoming." Holmes stopped to re-light his pipe.

"However," he continued, "I feel certain the gold is here In the Orange Free State. It may have already made it to Pretoria, but I don't think so."

"And the two heads?" It was like trying to draw teeth.

"Secret identity folderol. Duquesne has kept segments of his organization separate, but given them half pond gold coins with Kruger's head on both sides to identify each other. Quite melodramatic." He took another puff.

"Ponds?"

"The ZAR equivalent of our pound."

We sat quietly for a few moments each with our own thoughts.

"Any description of Duquesne, yet?"

"No Watson, quite the elusive creature. But fear not." He stood to go. "We shall have him yet. I've no doubt that he is the brains behind both the loss of information and the gold." He turned to walk off and called over his shoulder, "Interesting, Doctor. I shall inform my readers. Stay in touch." Off he went down the road.

The rest of the day was spent in preparing for more patients. Evidently the enteric had first been contracted at Paardeberg before the soldiers arrived in Bloemfontein. The bad water here only made things worse. Our problems were compounded by incessant rain. Before we left, one in five soldiers had enteric, and there were 1800 more shallow graves. It was so bad that no wood could be found to construct coffins and the men were buried in their brown blankets.

Early in the evening, I went in search of Mr Cacy. If he was making the rounds of the farms for hotels and boarding houses, he might be able to get milk for the hospital. I found him behind Mrs Foster's boarding house. He was alone and washing down his wagon.

"Mr Cacy," I started, "good evening. I've a question to ask you."

"Evening, doctor. I don't know if I'll have an answer, but you may ask." He threw his horse brush in the water bucket.

"Since you make the round of farms, do you know if there is milk to be had?"

"Milk, is it? Well, some I'm sure, but not much. And if it's to be had, it won't be cheap, but for you I'm sure I can find a bit."

"It's not 'a bit' that I want, I'm afraid." I went on to explain to him the critical nature of the need, probably at more length than he needed or wanted to know.

When I finally stopped, Cacy assured me he understood the what and why of my request.

"Sure, sir. You may need to come about with me and explain yourself to the farmers and use your silver tongue. I'm sure you'll convince them. But the price may be not to your liking."

I agreed to his proposal and he said he would let me know if he failed and take me around if necessary.

This was at a time when the Boer farmers or their families were still on the land. A few months later, when Lord Kitchener had taken over from Lord Roberts, the situation would be wholly different. The farms would be burned to the ground and the families in concentration camps. The earth would be scorched. But for now, I would be able to make some agreement with the farmers.

Chapter 12

A MURDER

Come the morning, Holmes had returned to the hospital and was standing with me as we watched Cacy pass the Rambler's Club grounds on his rounds. He waved and I returned it.

"I'll do what I can, doctor." He called. I smiled and waved again.

"Tell me about your friend down there, Watson."

"Not much to tell," I replied. I expressed what I knew about the man, even to his habit of washing his wagon daily.

"Most interesting," replied my companion when I had finished. "And what are your thoughts on Lieutenant Murtry?"

"Seems to be a good man. Dragoon Guards, good family. He is in a bit of a bad spot. Two masters you see." I went on to explain the awkward situation in which he found himself. "He also has a personal theory about what is going on."

"Has he shared it with you?"

"No, all he would tell me is that it involves canned goods, two kinds of potato diggers, and Sarvins. Whatever that all means."

"Hmm," sighed Holmes looking down the road after the disappearing wagon.

Holmes started to the stairs which went below. "The hospital is short-handed now, I hear."

"Yes, O'Callaghan has left, but I understand a Dr Schwartz is coming in and we will be getting two Sisters of Mercy, nursing sisters, to help. They're quite wonderful."

"Our friend Churchill seems to be everywhere nosing into things," Holmes continued as we exited the pavilion. "Not only attached himself to a colonial unit, but sending some blistering reports to his newspaper. I believe I've met him on two occasions, so I need to keep out of his way. If he sees you he'll undoubtedly ask about me. He has a suspicious nature."

"I assure you, Mr Holmes is home!" I grinned.

I took a cigarette from my case and tapped it on the lid. "I met a most fascinating man the other day, an American named Burnham. Scout, it seems. Well thought of too. We might think about using him, Holmes. If something is out of the ordinary, I believe he'll spot it."

"Yes. I've met him and Fredericks who, they have recently hired."

"Saw Fredericks in passing." I replied. "Don't know much about him."

"Aside from the fact that he is a Boer, educated in England, an excellent shot, been wounded at least twice, once in the left shoulder, once in the left foot, spent time in East London and Paris, neither a cricket nor a rugby fan, is partial to Turkish cigarettes, and quite the ladies' man, I know nothing."

"And his shoe size?" I muttered.

"Nine and a half," said Holmes taking a drag on his cigarette.

"Never mind," I chortled. "Sorry I asked."

A young private of mounted rifles thundered up to where we stood and reigned in his sorrel mare.

"Sir," he saluted, "where can I find Dr Doyle?"

"Inside private, may I help you? Are you injured?"

"No sir. Been a murder, sir, and I'm to get the Doctor straight away."

"Murder? Where?"

"At the headquarters, sir. The hotel, that is, upstairs.

"Alright Private, I'll inform Dr Doyle that he is wanted."

"Thank you, sir," responded the private and saluted again. As he was about to depart, Holmes called out, "Who was murdered, soldier?"

The private looked back. "Lord Roberts' aide, sir, Lieutenant Murtry." With those words he put spur to horse and rode off.

"Quickly, Watson! We must go to Lord Roberts and explain who I am. I must see this room before it is disturbed."

"I'll get Doyle. Lord Roberts sent for him" I looked about. "Moyer," I bellowed, "get me that ambulance." I pointed to a wagon being hitched by two of our St. John's men. "I'll be right back, Holmes."

In a few moments, Doyle, Holmes and I were on board the ambulance moving at a brisk pace toward the headquarters.

"Doyle," instructed Holmes, "you must go straight to Lieutenant Murtry's room. Under no circumstances let anyone touch anything. Do you understand?"

"Quite, Holmes. Fear not, I'll see to everything."

We had barely reached the hotel when the three of us bounded down from the ambulance and rushed for the door.

"Where is Lieutenant Murtry's room?" demanded Doyle of a sentry at the bottom of the stairs as Holmes and I turned right toward Lord Robert's Office.

Major Pelham was outside Lord Roberts' door as we approached.

"Lord Roberts is too busy to see the press this morning, Mr Escott. You know we had an accident here this morning and he is far too busy to see anyone."

Holmes pushed me forward toward Pelham which moved him to the side. I nearly fell into the door when it opened. "Pelham, get me Dickworth in here!" shouted Roberts.

"Yes, sir." replied Pelham.

"Your Lordship, I have come with Dr Doyle and Dr Watson. May I speak to you in private for a moment?" Holmes piped up and at the same time forcing his way through the door.

"I've no time for you Escott. There is too much going on. Pelham get this man out of here." With that Roberts tried to shut the door.

"Sir, I would suggest you look at this." Holmes held a paper before Roberts' face.

"What is this nonsense?" Roberts looked a moment then took the paper from Holmes. "Come in, sir," he said more calmly. As he closed the door he looked back at Pelham. "And get me Dickworth!" he shouted.

It seemed like forever, but in all probability was not more than five minutes, before the door reopened and Holmes came out.

"Where's Dickworth?" the voice inside bellowed as Holmes closed the door.

"His Lordship is not happy," whispered Holmes. "Not with me, not with you and definitely not with Whitehall! He does not appreciate being kept in the dark in his own command."

We were exiting Pelham's outer offices as I asked, "Are you to investigate?"

"Yes," replied Holmes, "but not exactly with his blessing."

We turned to the stairs and headed for Murtry's room.

Chapter 13

THE MURDER ROOM

Holmes and I found Doyle in the room above in quiet discussion with Major Parker, Lord Roberts' Intelligence Officer. On seeing us, Doyle advised that with the Major's help he had convinced everyone to leave the room.

"Should we go in?" Doyle asked.

"In a moment," replied Holmes, looking up and down the hallway. Half a dozen soldiers stood by waiting the Major's directions.

The hallway consisted of a dozen rooms on each side with windows facing the main road or the street behind. Lieutenant Murtry's room was second from the end on the right once one came up the stairs and turned left. His room would face the back street.

"Right," said Holmes, "lets' take a look inside."

We entered the room behind Holmes like a line of ducks. Holmes, myself, Doyle and Parker. Holmes stopped mid-way into the room. "Lestrade's men could not have done worse." He remarked. "Everyone stand still for a moment plcasc."

We all watched as Holmes circled the room. He leaned over the body lying on the bed for only a moment, then stepped back to scan the area around it. Slowly he studied the carpet and walked to the window looking out on the back street, came back to the left side and rattled the connecting door to the next room. It was locked.

"Who is in the next room?"

"Why, that's my room, Mr Holmes." replied Parker.

"You heard nothing in the night, Major?"

"Hardly, sir, I wasn't here. I was out on a scout with Captain Burnham. I just got back an hour ago. No sooner walked in than I heard all this commotion. An orderly had been sent to find the Lieutenant. When he couldn't get an answer at the door, he opened it. Thought the Lieutenant was sleeping, but when he went to wake him, he saw the blood and gave the alarm."

"I see." Holmes pondered a moment. "Major, would you be good enough to go around and open this door, while Dr Watson inspects the body? Thank you, sir."

I came forward and looked closely at the Lieutenant. "Why didn't you tell me what you were up to?" I muttered to the corpse.

"Don't blame yourself, Watson. You cannot control the actions of others." Holmes patted my shoulder. "What can you tell me about the wound?"

"Single deep thrust to the heart. Death was quick, but not instantaneous as they say in the novels. He had time to know he'd been murdered."

"And the weapon?"

"Ah, as to that, I'd say it was a bayonet. Not a usual kitchen knife or something. See how the top of the wound is wide and has a flat look to it and the bottom is thin and angular."

"Could it have been a hunting knife?" Doyle asked.

"Yes, possibly, but I'm more inclined to think bayonet. A hunting knife would probably give a taller wound."

"I see," said Holmes.

Parker had re-joined us by this time and the connecting door stood open. Holmes turned, and, studying the carpet, strode into the major's room and over to the windows.

There were two windows in the room. One looked out on the back street behind the building and the other to the alleyway to the East. Holmes then looked about the rest of the room. It was appointed much like Murtry's -

bed, nightstand, chest of drawers and a small writing table with a single chair.

"Major, can you send for whatever sentries were on duty last night at the bottom of the stairs and have them come here?" inquired Holmes.

"Certainly, sir. I'll be right back." With that reply, Parker left.

Doyle walked over to the windows and looked out.

"Can't say as I see anything, Holmes. What are you looking for in here?" asked the big man.

"Exactly what I knew I would find," smiled my friend. "But we'll wait for the major to get back; he'll have to report to Lord Roberts." Holmes walked back into Murtry's room and lighted a cigarette. A few minutes later, Major Parker returned with a young private who looked both sheepish and tired, and not at all sure what was about to happen to him.

"This is Private Morris, Mr Holmes," introduced the major. "He was on duty from midnight to four. I have another man looking for his replacement."

The private had stood to attention on entering the room. Holmes, always able to put people at their ease if he felt the situation required it, came up and put his hand on the boy's shoulder.

"My good sir, all I need to know is who went up the stairs last night during your watch. You're a good soldier; you can remember that, can you not?"

Private Morris seemed to relax a bit.

"Why, yes, sir. Just the usual people. By the time I come on most of the officers are already upstairs, so I only see a few."

"Well, then," Holmes took his hand down, "who were our late arrivals?"

"About one o'clock, there was General Kitchener, sir. But about ten minutes later comes Major Pelham and Captain Dunn." Morris leaned toward Holmes and in his best stage whisper said, "They was a bit done-up, if you know what I mean, sir." He looked sideways at Parker, who just stared back. Morris came back to attention. "That was it, sir. Didn't see nobody else until my relief came."

"Fine, thank you private," replied Holmes. "Would you be good enough to relay that I do not need to see your replacement after all? Excellent. Good day, private."

Morris saluted and left the room.

"Watson, can you give me a time of death?"

I looked at my watch. "Based on the body, I'd say it was between one and two in the morning, but you could stretch it an hour one way or the other."

Holmes walked over and sat on the bed with the body while he lighted another cigarette. We all stood quietly for a few moments and then Major Parker could take it no longer.

"Well, Mr Escott, what shall I tell Lord Roberts you have found?"

"First," started Holmes, "that the lieutenant was not murdered in this room."

"What? Where was he murdered?"

"Why in your room, of course."

"My room?"

"Quite. He was murdered in your room and then carried back in here and placed in his bed."

"But how do you know that?"

"It was obvious when we entered this room, Major. Look around. What is out of place?"

We all three looked about us until Holmes sighed and shook his head.

"What side of the bed is the body?"

"The left."

"And where are his book and the lamp?"

"On the right!"

"Murtry was right handed, if I remember correctly. So it does not make sense he would put himself to bed on the side away from his book and light. Therefore, someone else must have placed him there." Holmes strode to the centre of the room. "And here, sir, see how these foot marks are so deep in the carpet? And they come from where?"

"Through the connecting door," shouted Doyle, pointing at the next room.

"But why should he be in my room?" asked Parker.

"What does your room have that his does not?" replied Holmes. Parker shrugged.

"A fire escape onto the alley, Major." Holmes pointed to the second window, the one that emptied out onto the alleyway. "Lieutenant Murtry needed to use your room to secretly meet with someone. Someone he hoped would give him information, but instead gave him a knife in the heart."

"But there should have been some sign of blood," I protested.

"There is Watson. There are brown stains on the window sill and outside on the fire escape landing. I'll warrant the maid is short some towels when she does the rooms today."

"All you say makes complete sense, Holmes. I just wish we knew who did it."

"But we do, Watson."

"Holmes? I thought your name was Escott, sir?" It was Parker. I had spilled the beans, as they say. I was mortified.

"Don't worry Watson. Too many people were getting to know our little secret anyway." Holmes turned to the Major. "Yes Major, my name is Sherlock Holmes. Lord Roberts knows of my identity, but we are trying to keep as few people in the know about that as possible. I'm sure I can rely on your discretion."

"Certainly, sir. Now I understand why Lord Roberts sent you up here."

"Can we get back to your knowing who the murderer is, Holmes?" I blustered trying to change the subject.

"We know by this." Holmes held up a short length of watch chain. On the chain was what appeared to be a ZAR half-pond coin with two heads.

Holmes slipped it back in his pocket before I could look at it closely. "Found it by the window. Evidently pulled off going in or out."

"But why move the body, Holmes?"

"Just to give the murderer more time to get away and establish an alibi. What if the major had come back early? No, the body had to be moved."

"What do we do now?"

"I, Watson, am going to ask the major here to allow me to go through the Lieutenant's papers. Perhaps he wrote something down. As for you and Dr Doyle, I suggest the hospital has need of you both."

Once again, Holmes was correct.

Chapter 14

MILK RUN

Around mid-afternoon, Mr Cacy arrived at the hospital with his wagon. On it were a few cans of milk, for which I was very grateful. It did not, however, nearly meet our requirements.

"Is there more milk out there to be had, Mr Cacy, or is this all that we can hope for?"

"Ah, doctor. There's more sure, but for a price. It's a war-time economy and like I told you, the farmers are not trusting. I had to leave extra money on a promise to bring back these cans. Now, if you could give me the cans, it might help."

"I'll find what I can," I assured him. "May I come with you tomorrow? Perhaps I can convince these good people how critical all this is, not only to the army, but to the civilians."

"You could get us both killed wearing that uniform of yours, Doctor. I'll get you some clothes that won't stand out." He looked me up and down and shook his head. "But if you get me killed, me mother will never forgive you." Cacy flicked the reins and called for his mules to 'walk on'. "I'll get you those clothes this evening, Doctor," he called over his shoulder.

I did not see Holmes that night. I'm sure he was busy tracking Lieutenant Murtry's movements of the day before.

Holmes had come by to see me off on my adventure that next morning. We had drunk coffee while waiting for Cacy to appear. We watched as Cacy stopped at the hospital to retrieve his empty milk cans.

"Watson, I am going to ask you to be on your best behaviour today."

"What are you talking about?"

I want you to get as much information as you can from your new friend. One never knows what tit-bit of information may be of use and he travels everywhere."

I took leave of Holmes and descended to greet Cacy and climbed up on the seat beside him.

"Why you clean up real nice you do, doctor," he exclaimed, with a smile. "You look quite the proper Boer."

True to his word, he had provided me with 'less offensive clothing' - slouch hat, waistcoat, trousers and a sack coat large enough to hide an elephant. I'm sure I looked quite ridiculous.

Holmes waved from my spot on the roof and called down. "Remember."

"Why, what does your friend mean, doctor?"

"Oh, just to look for some fresh fruit if it's to be found."

Cacy nodded. "Not much likely there, sir."

We rode on in silence.

We were not more than twenty minutes beyond the picket lines when Cacy made his first stop. It was a small, pleasant-looking farm with a fair sized house, barns, outbuildings and corrals. Among the livestock were only four or five milk cows. This was our first stop. Cacy called out in a loud voice for someone to come meet us. An old man and a boy appeared from the barn and a woman of middle age came to the door of the cottage.

The boy ran forward and held the bridle of the offside lead mule (I think that was Anna) as we climbed down.

"Mr Van der Loot, this here is a doctor from town. He'd like to talk to you. I've got your cans in the wagon. I'll get them for you." Cacy turned to go to the back of the wagon.

"Aye, no one sick here, sir. We've no need." The old man looked at me with the inherent mistrust of a Boer for an outlander.

"No, sir, I know that, but you were kind enough to supply some milk to us and I see you have four or five fine milk cows, so I want to make an offer to buy all your milk if I can. I'll supply the cans if that would help."

"I don't know," replied the farmer. "Our own people have need of the milk, too."

"Mr Van der Loot, I have hundreds of men who are very ill. Many will die and there is nothing I can do about that. But some I can save. Some you can save. Men that you can send home to their families alive instead of leaving here dead."

"They'll be sent home, will they?"

"Yes." I agreed.

"I'll sell you all the milk I can, sir. If it will get these damned British out of here." The old man turned on his heels and headed for the barn.

"Gustaf, come help me," he called to the boy. "That Englishman can hold the mules."

This scene replayed itself in one form or another for eight more farms. We had half the wagon full of cans before we started back. We also had to find room for Cacy's usual load of produce.

It was at the third farm that I was surprised to find the two young men that I had seen before with Cacy, Seanan and Keenan. They helped us load a small amount of milk and corn when I heard Keenan ask Cacy if he had any canned goods to trade for the fresh corn and milk.

"Not today, boy," came the reply, "maybe tomorrow. Today you'll have to settle for silver." Keenan shrugged and looked at me with a curious resentment, or so I supposed.

As Cacy and I were returning that afternoon, Keenan's look kept coming back to me.

"I'm surprised," I remarked, "that those two Irish lads are not off on commando."

"Seanan and Keenan? No, not them. They work at the freight yard when trains come in and at night they make wagon parts in the barn behind Mrs Foster's. I don't know when they sleep. Wish I was that young again. Their sister Molly is Mrs Foster's maid."

We continued in silence until we got back to the hospital. Here Cacy saw to the unloading of the milk before going on to his usual rounds. Langman was there to pay him. I explained the arrangements I had made with the local farmers. Langman agreed to give Cacy funds each morning for the day's milk since the farmers would not agree to any other system.

I spent the rest of the day with our patients. In every soldier I looked at I saw myself lying in Kandahar sick with the same disease and delirium. It was the most horrible experience of my life.

It was well past nine o'clock that night that Holmes appeared. Doyle and I were sitting on one of the benches outside the pavilion trying to remove the stench of disease with the smell of shag tobacco. Holmes sat with us for a moment. We were all quiet.

"So, Mr Holmes, for I believe I may call you that now, what of the murder?" Doyle bit down on his pipe stem.

"Do not worry Dr Doyle, we shall prevail. But as you should know, there are other matters which need our attention more."

"More? More than the murder of that poor boy?"

"I assure you, Dr Doyle, the boy will be avenged. It is all part of a single plot, a plot that he got too close to. He should have confided in others. Instead, we will spend valuable time trying to find out what he knew."

We sat again for a moment.

"Where is Major Drury?" asked Holmes.

"I'd like to know the same thing, Holmes," responded Doyle. "Not doing his job as far as I can see. We see the man twice a day, morning and night, and never between. Were it not for Langman and Watson, no telling what state we'd be in."

"Yes, well, Watson would you care to accompany me? I've a few stops to make."

"Of course Holmes, if you need me."

"Go on," said Doyle. "I've got things here."

Holmes and I walked toward the main part of town.

"Where are we going, Holmes, or does it matter?"

"We are going to find your errant major and see what he knows. If I do not miss my guess, he is with Mrs Foster and should be quite in his cups by now. A perfect time for a discussion, is it not?"

"Where does he spend his days, Holmes?"

"He spends them with Major Pelham and trying to hob-nob with the general staff. I'm afraid he has reached the summit of his career, but he keeps trying to progress. It will not happen."

True to Holmes' prediction, Major Drury was both 'in his cups' and with the lady of the house. I could see them through the parlour window as we approached. I could also hear the ring of hammers on iron coming from the barn out back.

"It seems Mr Cacy's friends are busy making wagon parts," I advised.

"Really?" Holmes stopped for a moment and listened. "Yes, perhaps. Shall we knock?"

Taking the steps two at a time, Holmes rapped on the door. It was Mrs Foster who let us in.

"We are here to speak with Major Drury," stated Holmes as he brushed by the woman and walked into the parlour. I nodded, smiled and followed my friend. I did have time to notice how lovely the raven-haired mistress of the house was.

"Ah, Mr Escott, how are you. Haven't seen you since the trip over. Come in, come in."

Drury was definitely in a light mood.

"How is your reporting going, old boy? You'll get lots of copy soon. Lots of copy." His words were slurred and his tongue thick.

"Actually, major, we have been traveling under somewhat false pretences. Although I am reporting for the *Times*, my name is Sherlock Holmes, not Escott."

"Sherlock Holmes! Well what about that. And you, Doctor," he looked at me with a smile and wagged his finger, "I should have known. Where one goes, so goes the other.

"But I'm forgetting myself. A drink gentlemen?"

Holmes winked toward me. "Not for me thank you, but the doctor will have one."

Drury poured two whiskeys and handed me one. "Cheers."

"Well, what can I do for the famous Mr Holmes?" Drury leaned heavily on a settee.

"It seems," said Holmes, who had now seated himself, "that there is to be movement soon. As a reporter, I would be greatly helped if there is any information that you could share."

"With a reporter? No, sir. With a friend I might, but no, sir." He put a finger beside his nose. "I do have things I know you know." He laughed at some personal thought; the drink definitely had the better of him. And then he continued, "I won't tell just anybody."

"I can see that, sir and I will not press you." Holmes stood and turned to go. "Watson, if you've finished your drink, it's time we were off. Good night, Major."

I had to rush to keep up with Holmes passing Mrs Foster in the foyer and getting up with my friend only as he reached the bottom of the porch steps. Instead of turning down the road toward the hospital, Holmes went around the house, past the garden and toward the barn. Just as we approached it, Seanan and Keenan came out, each leading a saddled horse. Cacy was behind them.

"Shoeing tonight or making wagon parts?" I asked smiling and waving.

The two boys said nothing but mounted their horses and rode off toward the freight yard.

"Not very talkative tonight," I remarked to Cacy.

"Those two never are, Doctor. But they're good lads. They've got to go supervise the kaffirs unloading at the yard. Be a long night for them."

"You use keg shoes Mr Cacy?" Holmes spoke for the first time.

"Not me, but the boys there do. It's quicker, but not as good as far as I'm concerned. Are you a friend of the Doctor? I know I've seen you about."

"Yes, the name is Holmes. I'm reporting for the *Times*. Well, good night sir. Watson, we go in opposite directions I believe, but may I have a moment? Good night, Mr Cacy."

I wished Cacy a good night and Holmes and I walked to the road.

"Tell me, have we learned anything tonight?" I was feeling as though nothing had occurred.

"Watson, we have learned a great deal."

"We have?"

"We've learned that Major Drury will tell people whatever he knows. Which, of course, we already knew. He would have told us everything that occurred at the headquarters today with but the slightest help on our part. And we know that your Irish friends, whatever they were doing, were not shoeing horses."

"How do you know?"

"Watson, the only two horses in the barn were theirs and when they left it was easy to see that both horses had well-worn shoes. Cacy's mules were in the corral and had been since we went into the boarding house. So, whose horses were they shoeing?"

"But what was your question about keg shoes?"

"Cacy does not use keg shoes - you know, pre-made shoes that come in twenty five pound kegs. If he were shoeing, his hammer would make a dull thud as it hit hot iron. Keg shoes need not be heated and so make a ringing sound when shaped. They also require no forge be lit. If they were fabricating wagon parts the same would be true. Heated metal does not ring."

"So," I pondered, "if the boys were shoeing horses there would be a ringing sound. But they weren't shoeing because there were no new shoes. And the forge was burning, but didn't need to be. Do you understand all this Holmes?"

"Not yet, Watson. But I will. I have a meeting with Parker in the morning. Meet me there, eight o'clock."

Holmes hurried down the street toward the headquarters.

Chapter 15

THE INTELLIGENCE OFFICER

The following morning, I waved to Cacy as usual. Now, however, he was stopping to pick up empty milk cans and get funds from Lieutenant Langman. Our Boer friends had agreed to supply what milk they could, but only at a price paid daily.

I worked my rounds and by half seven, I started my walk to meet Holmes. I found him just going in to meet Major Parker when I arrived. The major took us straight away into his office and closed the door.

"Please, gentlemen, have a seat. Lord Roberts has already explained that you have full authority in the matter of Lieutenant Murtry's death, Mr Holmes. What can I do for you?"

"Major," started Holmes, "people who work closely together in trying circumstances get a feeling about their fellows. I would like your opinion on a few things."

"Of course, Mr Holmes, whatever I can do."

"Give me your opinion of Lieutenant Murtry."

"That's easy enough. Good man, fine family, well educated, loyal, hard worker. In short, Mr Holmes, I wish we had a lot more officers like him. Never a shirker. Kept his mouth closed, too."

"I see, and Major Pelham?"

"Yes, different sort there. He works hard, intelligent; don't really know anything about his family. He's very efficient, but, well, he somehow rubs people the wrong way."

"Does he have any particular associates?"

"Let's see, I believe he and Captain Dunn spend a close bit of time together, but since your chap Drury showed up," he nodded toward me, "he spends considerable time with him. I think he used to be sweet on his landlady, but she dropped him for Drury, so Pelham moved over here to the hotel. That's really about all I know."

Holmes sat quietly a moment then removed the coin and watch chain he had found in Murtry's room from his pocket.

"Tell me," he said handing the coin to Parker, "have you any ideas on this?"

Parker took the coin and examined it closely.

"Crudely made. Kruger's head on both sides. Copied from a '92 I'd say."

"Are you a numismatist, Major?"

"Oh, bit of an amateur, I guess. This coin was never made properly. They've taken a flan, that is, a blank, and stamped it without turning it into a planchet first."

The major saw my blank stare and smiling continued.

"You see, Doctor, first you make the blank or flan, then the blank is put in a collar to form an edge, then it is stamped. This coin was made by someone in a rush, or who doesn't understand the process." Parker handed the coin back to Holmes. I'm afraid that's all I can tell you about the coin. I've never seen another like it."

"Another thing, Major. What can you tell me about the 'Black Panther'?"

"I suppose it's no secret that we are looking for him. Everyone is. He's a man named Fritz Duquesne and he's a bad lot. Hates us with a passion. We believe he has a ring of spies that report through him to the Boer commandos. We've put £10,000 price on his head, but so far we've had no luck."

"Was Murtry doing something for you on Duquesne?"

"Mostly just keeping his eyes open. I wish he'd told me if he was really getting into something."

"Do you have any thoughts on who might have killed the boy?"

"No, Mr Holmes. I've thought a great deal about it, but I've no idea. I don't know anyone who disliked him." Parker thought a moment. "Mr Holmes, whoever killed Lieutenant Murtry did it because of what he had uncovered. I just don't know what that is."

"Another thing occurs to me, Major. Who is responsible for clearing the hiring of local men to work for the army?"

"There really is no clearing process, Mr Holmes. The units hire natives or white men as they see fit. In the headquarters, the junior aide would keep a record of names for those who worked here." Holmes' next question took me back a bit.

"What do you know about a man named Clint Cacy who brings produce to this hotel?"

"Yes, I know whom you mean. Good man. He spent six years in the Irish Rifles before coming to Africa to make his fortune, mustered out as a sergeant. Why? Have you anything I should know?"

"No, nothing at the moment, but I will keep you posted." Holmes rose from his chair. "Thank you, Major, you have been most helpful.

"Before I go, let me share this with you. I have reason to believe there is a leak in information coming from this headquarters. I don't know who yet, but Lieutenant Murtry found out something and didn't share it. Don't make the same mistake."

"I won't, Mr Holmes. But I also won't give testimony unless I'm sure of my suspicions."

Holmes and Parker shook hands. I followed suit and spoke for the first time.

"Major, I know how much Lieutenant Murtry thought of his gelding, Boy-O. I'd like to buy him so you can send the money to his family."

"Of course, Doctor. We normally auction off such things. We just send personal items home. I'll see what I can do; we might be able to arrange the sale. You'll pay premium for such a good horse, you know."

"That would be fine, sir. I'll take good care of him."

"Watson," said Holmes once we had taken our leave of the major, "I want to speak with Captain Burnham. Let us see if he is in his room."

Chapter 16

BOY-O GETS NEW SHOES

Burnham's room was on the same floor as Lieutenant Murtry's, but down the opposite end of the hallway. On Holmes' knock came that deep American voice calling us to enter. Burnham was standing by the window.

"Ah, Doctor, how are you? What can I do for you this morning? I was just about to head downstairs." He came forward and shook my hand.

"Captain, let me present my friend, Mr Sherlock Holmes."

"Sherlock Holmes!" exclaimed Burnham, shaking hands enthusiastically, "A pleasure, I assure you. Why you're quite famous in the States. Thanks to the doctor here."

"I know much of you also, Captain." replied Holmes.

"Not many places to sit down gentlemen, but grab a seat. What can I do for you?"

Holmes sat on a corner of the small table and I seated myself on the bed.

"Captain Burnham," started Holmes, "I have come to you, a man of impeccable reputation, because I need some insight which you may have."

"I'll help you in whatever way I can, of course, but what exactly do you need to know?"

"You have been here some time with the headquarters. What is your opinion of Major Parker?"

"Why, as far as I know he's a good man. I don't have any reason to distrust him. Just what are you getting at Mr Holmes? What is all this about?"

"Captain, I believe I can trust you and I need an ally within the headquarters. It is my job to stop the transfer of secret information that is occurring. The Boers are finding out our movements almost before the orders go out."

Holmes went on to explain all that had occurred. Burnham stood in rapt attention. When he had finished, he showed the two-headed coin and asked if Burnham had ever seen another like it.

"No, Mr Holmes, I have not. But what can I do to help?"

"Answer a few questions, if you would. Besides Major Parker, what are your thoughts on Majors Pelham and Drury, Captain Dunn and your new scout, Fredericks?"

"Pelham seems to be alright I guess. Bit stuck up, I think, but he backs Rhodes well enough. He drinks too much for me, as does the doctor's friend, Drury. He's a bit of a waster, but honest I'd say. Dunn I don't know very well. He's an operations officer, so he'd know plans ahead of time, and he drinks with Major Pelham, never to excess that I've ever seen. I don't drink myself."

Burnham stopped for a moment, obviously thinking.

"And Fredericks," prompted Holmes.

"Yes, I was just thinking about him. He's new, of course. I hunted and fought in this area for years. I've never heard of the man. But he's young; maybe 22 or 23, and I've been gone for some time. He's a first-class hunter and scout I've seen that. He was raised a Boer, but he speaks with an English accent. He went to school in England. If you want to know anything about him, just ask. He is definitely not shy about telling you about himself. Some of it is made, shall we say, bigger than life. But I've nothing against him and he never talks shop, just about himself."

"I believe we've taken up enough of your time, Captain. I know that I may rely on your discretion."

"I'm going on a scout with Fredericks tonight, Mr Holmes. Should anything untoward occur, I will let you know."

Shaking hands all around, Holmes and I left. It was now noon. I told Holmes I must get back to the hospital. For his part, Holmes wished to send off some telegrams and so we parted. To my good fortune, Cacy was delivering milk to the hospital as I arrived.

"Looks like you have the gift, Doctor. I've half a wagon of milk. If this keeps up, I'll have to get a second wagon just for you."

"I believe the convincing argument was the silver coins and not my silver tongue," I laughed.

I was about to walk on when I remembered something.

"Mr Cacy, I may have a new gelding this afternoon. Do you think you might be able to shoe him tonight?"

"I'm not like the boys, sir. I need some daylight, not lanterns. Bring him over before seven and we'll see what we can do."

I agreed and went back into the hospital while Cacy and a half dozen soldiers unloaded the wagon.

Later that afternoon came word from Major Parker that Boy-O would be mine. I must say a princely sum was asked, but I felt the gelding worth it. The bay was what I would call a "parade horse". He was sound, with four white stockings and a blaze. I judged him to be about ten years of age and of an even temperament. It was close on to half six when I finally got away to the stables. Fortunately Boy-O was taken daily care of by the headquarters stable detail, so my chores would be few.

As part of my agreement with Parker, he had included the tack in the price of the horse. Though a groom could have saddled Boy-O, I preferred to do it. There is a bond that must be forged between a man and his horse. That bond can be stronger than any human one. In Afghanistan I had seen more than one steed stand by the body of his fallen rider while confusion and battle raged around them.

Having saddled, I rode to the barn behind Mrs Foster's boarding house. Cacy was already there, as were his two friends, Seanan and Keenan.

"Ah, Doctor, right on time I see. You can give the horse to Seanan to hold. Keenan," he called, "get on that bellows for me like a good lad."

I dismounted. Handing the reins to Seanan, I followed them into the barn.

"Have a seat, Doctor. This won't take too long. We'll have you out of here within the hour." Cacy was pulling bar stock from off a shelf. He looked back at Boy-O and with a practiced eye decided on the size of the bars to bend.

Little was the discussion over the next hour as Cacy forged and hammered. I did notice what Holmes had mentioned, but I had never really thought of it before. Hot Iron does not ring. Instead it makes a dull sound as the almost-molten steel is formed.

I took the time to look around the inside of the barn. It looked the same as any other I had ever seen. Barrels, boxes, hay, harness and wheels were hung or laid about. By the forge itself were stocks of steel and some iron pots. There were all the usual tools of a blacksmith: forge tongues, vice, anvil, hardy tools. There were also piles of canvas and a complete repair kit for tents and tarpaulins. Along the wall were boxes of grommets and dies for the canvas and numerous coils of rope.

Cacy was an excellent farrier. In less than the promised hour, Boy-O had shiny new shoes.

"What is the bill, Mr Cacy? That is a fine job."

"Don't worry, Doctor, I'm happy to do it. There's no charge. But I'll tell you, next time the boys and I are at Yager's Hotel, we'll put a pint on your bill."

Laughing, I could only agree. Keenan came up to Boy-O and rubbed his neck.

"Doctor," said the young man, "you won't be here forever. When you leave, I'd sure like to have this fine animal."

His remark, though innocent enough, made me nervous. "Should you still be about when I leave, we may make an arrangement, but for now I think that such is premature."

"Just remember, Doctor. I'd take good care of him."

"Yes, well, good night. And Cacy, I'll tell the barman you're owed a few." So stating, I rode off.

It was just turning dark as I got to the stables. Holmes was there, along with Burnham and Fredericks.

The two scouts were saddled and about to depart. As I dismounted, Burnham and Fredericks both wished me a good evening and departed.

"Anything new, Holmes?" I inquired.

"No. But I believe we are making progress. And you, Watson, I see you've had your horse shod."

"Yes, Cacy is quite the excellent blacksmith. But, I must say that his two fellows make me nervous. I cannot but feel they are up to something. Could they be involved in your leak of information? They do work at the rail yard, after all. They see quite a bit."

"The answer, Watson is both yes and no. They could, of course, pass on information about stores and troop strength, but they would have no access to plans. No, if they are involved, they are merely couriers, not the spies we seek."

"Let me give Boy-O a quick brush, and I will buy us some refreshment. I need to put some money on the tab for Cacy. It was all he'd take."

"Excellent, Watson, we shall socialize and listen."

Chapter 17

THE SECOND MURDER

We may have listened at Yager's Hotel that night, but as far as I could tell, we heard nothing of any import.

The next morning, I was in the wards early making rounds, long before Cacy came for the milk cans. To my surprise, I found Burnham and Fredericks in the tent beside the entrance to the pavilion. This particular tent was used as a triage station to sort the critical from the ordinary. The two scouts seemed both the worse for their night of travel. Fredericks was sitting on a camp stool while Moyer stitched a long jagged wound in his left calf. Burnham was just watching the process. Both were dirty and obviously tired. Regardless of wound or lack of sleep, Fredericks was still cheerful.

"Good morning, Dr Watson," he cheerfully called as I entered.

"Some bad luck last night?" I queried. "Well, you could not be in better hands than Moyer here. What happened?"

"I think they were trying to kill us, Doctor. That's my opinion. What do you think Burnham?" Fredericks laughed as if he had made an exceptional jest.

Burnham stared at his fellow scout and, turning, left the tent without a word. There was something between these two men. Was it jealousy, envy, or just competition for favour in the eyes of Lord Roberts?

"Well, I must get back to work," I said. "You must tell me later what has happened. I'd be greatly interested."

"It's of no consequence, sir. We didn't get done what we wanted, but there's always tonight."

I left the tent to find Burnham outside. He was standing alone deep in thought when I approached.

"May I offer you a cigarette, Captain?"

He looked up at me and shook his head.

"No thank you, Doctor. I don't smoke. It's bad for your sense of smell."

With that I had to agree. Later I would find that besides not smoking and drinking, he ate very little and drank very little water. He asserted that he had learned this in his days fighting Indians. He trained his body to do without and therefore survived where others could not.

"What happened last night, Captain? Where are your horses?"

"Lost, sir, both of them. I hated to lose that little mare. She was a good one, Basuto pony you know." He shook his head again. "You know it is a truism that the English don't know how to take care of horses. The animals here should be in good shape by now. They're not."

"Some Englishmen do know how to take care of their horses, you know."

"Sorry, Doctor. Present company excluded of course." He took a deep breath. "We did exceedingly poorly last night."

"Sometimes one just doesn't have the right luck, you know."

"That wasn't it. We were moving too quickly. I wanted to slow our pace, but Fredericks insisted we hurry. He was afraid we would not make the kopjes we went to scout and return before sunrise. I admit it was going to be a close run thing, but you still must be cautious.

"At any rate, we were about five miles out when we came upon fresh tracks. Probably six or seven riders. They were going in the same direction as we were. By the stride I'd say there were at least two thoroughbreds. The rest were native ponies. It had to be Boers. I made Fredericks slow a bit, but about two more miles on we decided to cross the saddle between two kopjes. I guess there was a donga on the other side or a dry wash. At any rate, we were caught in it. The Boers jumped us and the shootin' was pretty fast.

"My mare went down almost immediately. We'd only been able to retreat a few hundred yards. I'll hand it to Fredericks; he came back, caught me up behind him and made a run for it. We'd gone down a steep slope when the horse lost his feet and we tumbled over into another dry wash. The drop must have been twenty feet. The horse, then Fredericks, then me. Poor beast had two broken legs. Nothing we could do but put him down. Fredericks had that gash on his leg, but I just had the wind knocked out. Landed on all that padding, I guess. But one thing I still don't understand."

"What's that?"

"Why didn't they come after us?"

"Perhaps they didn't want to fall in the dry wash." I laughed.

Burnham looked at me as if he was thinking deeply. Finally he threw up his hands.

"And perhaps you are correct, Doctor perhaps."

"How did you get back?"

"We walked. We'd have been back sooner except for Fredericks's wound. When we got to the line of pickets, we were able to find a wagon coming in.

"And now I really need to report in. I hate to report a failed scout. I take it very personally. Ah, Mr Holmes, good morning, sir."

I looked around to find my friend approaching up the walkway.

"Good morning, gentlemen. Captain Burnham, I believe that the headquarters has need of you. There is a bit of a crisis at the moment."

"What is going on, Holmes?" I asked.

"It seems that Major Parker has disappeared. No one has seen him since late yesterday."

"I had best be off, gentlemen," put in Burnham. "Doctor, will you tell Fredericks where I've gone?"

"Of course, sir, of course."

Burnham literally trotted down the road.

"Holmes, surely Parker has learned from Murtry's death. He hasn't done anything precipitous!"

"Watson, if there is one thing on which you may always count it is the folly of men. I fear he has done just what he was asked not to do. But come, let us go to the headquarters and see what progress has been made."

I sent a St John's man to Fredericks with Burnham's message then accompanied Holmes.

As we walked up the dusty road toward the centre of town, a spring wagon passed us. Whatever was in the back was covered with a pauline. Beside the wagon rode two men, both in colonial uniform. As they came abreast of us, one, a lieutenant, looked down at us then drew rein.

"Mr Sherlock Holmes, is it not, sir." It was a statement, not a question.

"And you, sir, are Winston Churchill. I don't believe we have ever been formally introduced, but allow me to present Captain Watson, Doctor, RAMC."

I nodded my head and proffered my hand. "Delighted, Lieutenant. I've read some of your works, very enlightening."

"And I yours, Doctor, very, ah, entertaining. I'd heard rumours that you were about, Mr Holmes. Whatever you are here for I'd appreciate being made part of. Still reporting, you know."

"Who is in the back of the wagon?" asked Holmes, ignoring Churchill's request.

My head snapped around to Holmes. "I saw the outline of a boot, Watson."

"I'm sad to say that it is Major Parker from the headquarters. My lads found him in a donga this morning out on the road to the Modder. Horse and equipment were gone." Churchill looked down the road where the spring wagon and his sergeant were disappearing into the distance. "I'd best catch up. Until later, gentlemen." He spun his horse around and with a nudge of the knees trotted after his men.

"Once again we are denied access to a crime scene, Watson."

"Now, Holmes, it wasn't really a crime scene. This is a war."

"No, Watson, I assure you, this was a murder. A cold, calculated murder. Let us get to the headquarters and see what we can find.

By the time we arrived, Churchill and his men had already departed and Parker's body had been placed in a shed behind the hotel.

Going to what had been Lieutenant Murtry's office, we met the lieutenant's replacement. He was older than Murtry had been. Lieutenant Barthelme had been a sergeant in the Royal Horse Artillery and received an offer of a commission because of his actions at Colenso, where Lord Roberts's son had met his death. To say the man looked uncomfortable would be an understatement. The change from file closer to lieutenant would take time.

On introduction, Barthelme shook our hands vigorously. It seemed he was a fan of my small works about Holmes.

"Lieutenant," started Holmes. "We have been engaged by Lord Roberts to investigate the death of your predecessor, Lieutenant Murtry. I believe that Major Parker's death may be related and I desire to inspect his body. Can you arrange that?"

"Oh, certainly, Mr Holmes. I was just about to go back there. I must account for his personal effects. Would you and the doctor like to come along?"

We entered a small shed behind the hotel. It was empty except for a single table in the middle of the room where Parker had been laid out.

"Take a look, Watson, and give me your medical opinion."

I approached the table and inspected the man's body finding nothing save four bullet wounds. One was in the neck, two in the chest and one in the abdomen.

"I'd say the neck wound would have been survivable. The other three were all mortal. The abdominal wound would have been a lingering death. In a sad way, it's fortunate the other two took him quickly."

"Can you tell what weapons may have caused the injuries?"

"No, Holmes, all of them exited the body. But I'd venture that they were of about thirty calibre." I could hear my own sigh. "Either side could have imposed these wounds. They were all fired from a distance. You can see there are no powder burns on the clothes or flesh. The only other thing I can say for certain is that he was facing his executioners at the time."

"If you are finished I must collect his things now, gentlemen." The lieutenant started to turn out the major's pockets as Holmes watched attentively. There was not much - a pencil, a few coins, a watch, around his neck a miraculous medal. But in one pocket there was a piece of paper. Barthelme looked at it then held it out to me. "It's for you, sir."

"Me?" I asked as I approached and took the missive. On the outside of the folded paper were the words, "Dr Watson". I unfolded the paper, read it and then handed it to Holmes.

"Supply wagons. Meeting scout. Will explain," was the entire note. It was signed, "Parker".

"What can this mean, Holmes?"

"I'm sure I don't know, Watson. Not yet. 'Supply wagons'- he used the plural not the singular."

"How is that significant?"

"Had it been singular, I believe it would confirm a hypothesis. But as it is, it seems to add a cloud of fog to our problem." Holmes handed back the note.

We thanked the new lieutenant and walked out into the sunlight. From where we stood, I could see the dust of the rail yard as scores of supply wagons made their way from the trains to the units carrying everything needed to keep an army in the field. Which wagons had Parker meant?

"Holmes he said 'meeting scout'. Burnham didn't mention anything about Major Parker. What scout was he meeting? It couldn't be Fredericks, he and Burnham were together all night."

"Yes, Watson, but Burnham has a whole section of scouts. I'll make inquiries, but I do not hold out much hope."

I spent the rest of my day at the hospital. The dead were being carried out constantly and grave digging had become a full time job for some.

Chapter 18

MRS FOSTER GETS A SHOCK

The next morning I hoped for two things: Relief from the new cases of enteric fever and some solution to our mysteries. The sun had barely risen when I heard Holmes's familiar tread coming up the steps to our roof. He drew out his pipe and joined me at what had become my 'thinking spot' at the roof's edge. Neither of us spoke for quite a long time as we watched the army awake to another day.

There were regular army men, colonials, yeomanry, Scots with their plaid kilts and khaki aprons, all going somewhere, all performing the functions of everyday life and the serious business of an army at war.

As we stood watching the road, a battery of the new Pom-Pom guns trotted by below.

"What type of weapon is that, Watson? It seems to be a very large machine gun."

"You've fairly well described it, Holmes. It's a 37mm automatic cannon. Fires a one-pound shell from a belt of, I think, twenty-six. It's kind of an oversize Maxim gun. It's new to us, but the Boers have been using them all along. To great effect too, I might add. Doesn't do a lot of damage, but the effect of all that fire coming in on one makes one slow down and re-think whether or not one wants to charge into it. Very effective. I'm glad we finally have some." I started to tap out my pipe on the wall. "I'm afraid Mr Milner underestimated our Boer friends and their preparations."

Holmes was busy re-lighting his pipe. "What type wheels are on the carriages of those guns?" He asked between puffs.

"Wheels?" I looked at the last of the guns moving rapidly away from us. "Sarvins, I believe."

"And what had Murtry said? He referred to Sarvins, did he not?"

"Yes, he did, Holmes, but most wheels these days are either Sarvins or Archibalds. That's pretty standard."

"Interesting. Spoke to your Major Drury last evening at some length. He is really a pretty good fellow when not in his cups."

"Yes, he's not a bad sort. He has really pitched in here during the day of late. But the nights are his, I assure you."

"It seems, Watson, that he much resents this particular duty as liaison with a civilian hospital. He feels very keenly he should have been assigned to a forward unit."

"I can understand that. You always want to be where there is action."

"He is also quite smitten with Mrs Foster. It is not just a casual thing with him. I believe he actually thinks he's in love with her."

"Ah, Holmes. One does not 'think' they are in love. It is a feeling; it is an emotion, not a thought process."

Holmes puffed a moment.

"No doubt you are right, Watson. But in any event, he spends each night drinking and telling his life story to the woman. I fear, however, he is to be disappointed in his affair de coeur. She is in love with Pelham."

"Holmes, how could you possibly know that?"

"Oh, it's just a feeling, Watson." Holmes smirked and looked down as Cacy pulled his wagon to a halt beside the pavilion to load empty cans.

"And those wheels, Watson, they are which?" Holmes pointed at the wagon.

"Archibalds, no, they are Sarvins. But, as I said, they are so common I don't know how that information will help us."

"I don't know yet, Watson, but we shall see, we shall see." Holmes tapped out his pipe and started for the stairs.

"Four o'clock Watson, at the hotel. Be there, my boy. I've things to do in the meantime and so have you."

This day was as bad as the rest. We now had one hundred and sixty men in our little hospital for fifty. The excess made our sanitary conditions as bad as any I had seen in Afghanistan twenty years before. So, I shamefully admit, it was almost with relief that at half three I started my walk to meet Holmes. It was as I was leaving that Cacy and his mates arrived.

"Stand now, Victoria, Anna! Stand now." He called out.

"And what are the names of the other two?" I called up to Cacy.

"Oh, they'd be Polly and Pattie, but they're good wheelers. They'd much rather stand, you know. It's the lead that always wants to do something." He jumped down from the box and patted Polly as men came to unload the milk. "Of course, if all I ever saw was blinkers and a mule's ass, I wouldn't want to walk on either." He and I both laughed.

Cacy looked toward the pavilion. "It's sad, these men, you know. If they'd never come here, they wouldn't die here." He took a deep sigh. "Right, then. They've unloaded, can I take you somewhere?"

"No, Mr Cacy. Thank you, but I'd like to walk."

Cacy tipped his hat, and, climbing back up on the box, flicked his reins and called "Walk on" as I started my way to the headquarters.

As I came up on the headquarters, I saw Captain Burnham approaching from the opposite direction. We met at the walkway to the veranda.

"Another scout last night, Captain?"

"Hello, doctor. Yes, every night right now."

"How is Fredericks?"

"He's fine. That scratch won't slow down a good scout. Hello, Mr Holmes."

Holmes had come out on the veranda to join us.

"Captain, anything of interest last night?"

"Well, I can't really discuss exactly what I find, Mr Holmes, let me say I saw the same men as the night before, but this time I could skirt them no problem. One man can move much better than two. Don't get me wrong. Fredericks knows what he's doing, it's just easier."

"Do you think we'll ever move on the water works?" I inquired.

"I hope so, Doctor. From what I can see they aren't putting much effort into holding onto it. I think we should move now. But I guess Lord Roberts knows what he's doing."

Holmes approached the captain to ask his next question.

"Would it be possible for me to accompany you on a scout, Captain?"

"Depends, Mr Holmes. I wouldn't want to jeopardize the scout or you. Maybe if it's nothing too serious. You have a good horse?"

"No, but I have a friend with one." Holmes looked straight at me.

"Yes, Holmes. You may borrow Boy-O, but nothing better happen to him, or you."

"All right, Mr Holmes, be ready by eight. I'll let you know then if I can take you. But what are you looking for?"

"Information. Come, Watson, we must hurry down to Mrs Foster's. Good day, Captain. Until eight then, at the stables."

I wished the captain a good day and, as usual, hurried to catch up with Holmes.

"Why Mrs Foster's?" I puffed out as we hurried down the street.

"The barn behind, actually. I want to inspect it before Cacy finishes his deliveries or Major Drury comes back from the hospital."

Reaching the barn in question, Holmes called out in a loud voice for anyone there to come out, we wanted to talk to them. There was no reply, so we entered.

"Watson, stay at the door and let me know if anyone is coming."

"Right, Holmes. But what are you looking for?"

"As I told the good Captain, I seek information."

I admit that I was half watching the roadway and half watching Holmes. He held his hand over the forge, which still retained heat from its use the night before, then he started in a clockwise direction around the inside of the building. He checked the iron pots, the blacksmith tools, the empty wooden crates, the empty stalls and the spare canvas. He took out the canvas repair kit, looked at the dies and rawhide hammer and rummaged through the grommet boxes. Finally he started an inspection of the harness hanging along the north wall.

After what seemed an eternity, he came out of the barn.

"Curious."

"What is curious, Holmes?"

"There must be four sets of team harness and another three saddles and bridles in that barn, but only one bridle has polished rosettes. Why would a man only polish one set of rosettes?"

"Perhaps he only had time to polish one. Or perhaps that bridle has a special meaning." I offered.

"Of course it has a special meaning, Watson. The question is - what is that special meaning?"

"Is there something I can do for you gentlemen?"

I nearly jumped. The voice belonged to Mrs Foster. She had approached as Holmes and I were lost in thought.

"Ah, Mrs Foster. Dr Watson and I were just looking for Mr Cacy."

"He should be back any time now, Mr Holmes. Would you like to come in and wait for him?"

"No, thank you, my dear lady. I know you are quite busy with your duties. We will come back later. Come, Watson, I promised to help Major Pelham pick out a gift to send his wife for their anniversary and I don't want to disappoint the man."

Mrs Foster touched Holmes's arm. There was an anxious look in her face. "Mr Holmes, I'm afraid you are much mistaken. Major Pelham is not married."

"No, my good woman, I'm afraid he is. She lives in Sussex with their son, Timothy."

"But that can't be, sir. Why he said…" The woman was now completely distraught. With visible effort she gathered herself. "Excuse me, gentlemen. I have things I must do." Mrs Foster turned and went up toward the house.

"Holmes," I admonished once the woman was out of ear shot. "That was cruel. Is it even true?"

"Yes, Watson, it was the response to one of the telegrams I had sent."

"But why be so cruel and tell her in such a callous way?"

"I am stirring the pot, Watson. It may produce nothing, but I think it may bring us some good yet."

"I hope you are correct."

"Watson, I wish to send some additional telegrams. Would you inform Captain Burnham that I will

143

not be going with him tonight? Good fellow. I will see you later tonight."

I did not see Holmes later that night as promised, but did receive a note from him. "We have been invited to meet with Mrs Foster at nine tomorrow morning. Holmes"

His assumption I had nothing else to do was always irritating, but I knew I would attend.

Chapter 19

THE THIRD MURDER

I awoke late that morning. I had been up until almost dawn working in the wards. It was the clanging of the milk cans that awakened me. It was fortunate they had, for Holmes was already present and sitting quietly on a box near my bunk, smoking.

"Good morning, Watson. It's time you were up and about, is it not?"

"I've just gone to bed, thank you." I turned over onto my back and sat up rubbing my eyes. I could see Doyle just coming up the stairs.

"Holmes," bellowed the big man. "I understand we use your correct name these days."

"Yes, Doctor. No need for subterfuge except to my true mission. How is the hospital?"

"This is disastrous, Holmes. About one in six soldiers is ill and I can't get Roberts to make a move. It's a disgrace." Doyle drew in a deep breath. "You can smell our problem." He exhaled. "But how goes your investigation?"

"Not well either, I'm afraid. We are making progress. I hope it will not be too late when we find an answer." Holmes looked to me as he continued. "Get your boots on, Watson; we shall get you something to eat before we make our appointment."

"I really cannot go. There is too much to be done here. You'll have to get on without me, I'm afraid."

"As you wish, Watson. I can see you are needed. I will keep you posted. Gentlemen, good day."

He was gone as I pulled my boots from under my bunk. I and two or three others were the only ones still living on the roof. Doyle had gotten a room shortly after our arrival.

"I'll be down in a minute, Doctor. Was there anything you needed?"

"No, I saw Holmes coming up and thought I'd find out how things were. See you below." Doyle left as I gathered my things.

Despite my best intentions, I was not destined to spend my morning with patients. To our great good fortune, our little hospital was bolstered that very morning by the arrival of two Catholic Nursing Sisters. These women were true angels of mercy and I can never express how much they meant to us or how hard they worked. In the coming weeks, there seemed never to be a time when I was in the hospital, that they were not there tending to the sick and wounded. But I go off on a tangent.

Hardly had I reached the ward when Major Drury accosted me. The man was shaking and tears were running down his face. He leaned heavily on the door frame of the entryway.

I rushed to the man's aide when I saw him. His legs were wobbly and I pulled over a stool and sat him upon it.

"Take a breath, man. What has happened?"

"Mr Holmes needs you, Doctor! He needs you now." Drury gripped my arm with his trembling hand.

"Drury, get a hold of yourself." I said sternly. "Then tell me what has happened."

The major took a gulp of air. "She's dead! Murdered! The bastards have blown her head off." He fell to weeping again.

"Who, Drury, who has been killed? Is it Mrs Foster?"

"Yes, Watson. We couldn't find her this morning. But when Mr Holmes arrived," he sobbed, "when Mr Holmes arrived, we found her in the garden, dead. The side of her face was gone. It was horrible." Drury dropped his head in his hands.

Leaving Drury to Moyer, I hurried on to the boarding house where I found Holmes, the Bloemfontein Constabulary and Lieutenant Barthelme.

"I know we are under Martial Law here Lieutenant, but this is a civilian and a matter for the Constabulary to deal with. Don't you agree, Mr Holmes?"

"Normally I would, Inspector. But as the lieutenant says, this murder may have other aspects. I'm afraid I must agree with him. Perhaps you should discuss this with major Pelham at headquarters."

"I assure you I will sir," replied the inspector in a heavy Boer accent. "We are not an English Colony, yet!" The inspector stormed off down the road.

"I do not believe you've made a friend there, Holmes." I chided.

"Watson, good. Come tell me what you can of this wound."

The body lay in the middle of a small garden. The woman was in a nightgown and a brown robe. No wonder she had been overlooked in the dim morning light. Kneeling down I examined her head.

"Why, she's been bludgeoned to death, Holmes. This is not a gunshot wound as Drury supposed."

"No, Watson. I believe that blacksmith's hammer behind you will prove to be the instrument of death. Can you say how long ago?"

"Well, the body is in complete rigor, so not less than eight hours."

"That would put it between midnight and one, you would say?"

"Yes, but it's never an exact science." A shadow fell across the body and I looked up. It was Drury. He seemed to have gathered himself together.

"I'm sorry I hadn't control of myself, Watson." He started. "It seemed so fiendish. And to leave her out here in the open... Who does such a thing?"

"We intend to find out, Major, but I need you to answer some questions."

Holmes had come forward, and taking Drury by the arm, led him to the barn. I asked Lieutenant Barthelme to have his men remove the body, then joined Holmes.

"When did you last see Mrs Foster?" Holmes asked the man.

"Let's see, it would be about eleven, I think. She was most distracted all evening. Something was preying on her, but she would not tell me what it was."

"Yes, I see." Holmes gave me a knowing look.

"Did anyone come to see the lady?"

"Not from eight o'clock on. We were together until I went upstairs."

"Anyone unusual about the place?"

"Not that I noticed. There was the usual working going on in the barn, but those men left about ten or so. They usually leave about then and go to one of the hotels. They're the only establishments allowed to sell drinks."

"Alright. Thank you, Major. I think it would be best if you went up to the house."

"I think I'll go to the hospital, if you don't mind. I've some things I should be taking care of." With a look to where the lieutenant's men were loading the body on a spring wagon, Drury shuffled out toward the road.

"Is there anything else you can tell me, Watson?"

"Didn't want to say it in front of Drury, but I believe she was attacked from the rear with that hammer. The blow came to the right side, in the temple area. But the heavy crushing is toward the back. She was hit from behind, Holmes."

"So, we have a right handed man whom she knew and did not fear or was surprised by."

"In the quiet of the night with the foliage and dead grass? She could not have been surprised surely."

"You are correct, of course, Watson. But one should look to all possibilities before discarding any out of hand."

"Of course. Did you find anything before I got here?"

"Nothing much. The poor lady was allowed to fall where she was attacked. The body was not moved from somewhere else."

"Any footprints?"

"Far too many, Watson. Besides her own, there were none that I could say were directly associated. And those that were there were all plain leather. Not so much as a sole with a hole in it like Mr Cacy's."

"You noticed that?"

"Oh, yes."

"So you've no clue as to who did this?"

"I have one, my friend. I have this." Holmes held up a woman's fob watch, the kind worn by nurses, nuns and housekeepers. It was the kind that pins to an apron with the watch face showing 12 at the bottom, so a woman might look down and tell the time.

"It was on Mrs Foster's robe. I took it off. Do you notice anything curious about it?"

Holmes handed me the watch. It was a good, sturdy watch. Heavy for its size and nickel plated. The fob pin had an inscription, *"Facilis est Descensus Averni."*

"The decent to hell is an easy one," I mumbled. "What an odd inscription for a watch."

"It is not so odd, really. But look at the back."

I turned the watch over. On the back was the head of Kruger, the same as on the coin we had seen. "Holmes!"

"Open it, Watson. On the inside is the second head." And it was.

"So Mrs Foster was part of the spy ring?"

"Certainly, but I believe she was only a messenger and provided a safe place for men to stay."

"So is Drury involved? I can't believe it. Why would he be? He came with us. How would that explain the gold or the spying before we got here?" I handed the watch back to Holmes.

"I really don't know, Watson. But we must make progress and soon. But come, you must get back to the hospital and I must think. I will walk with you."

We walked quietly as my mind raced. Who had killed the poor lady? She was our enemy, but loyal to her Boer roots. "Holmes, surely Pelham would not do such a thing. I mean, Mrs Foster was quite upset, but even if she confronted him he would not stoop to murder."

"Who knows what one would do when faced with the threat of destruction to one's career? So we must not rule him out - or Drury for that matter."

"Have you found out who Parker was going to meet on the road to the Modder?"

"Neither Burnham nor Fredericks nor any other of the scouts claim the honour I'm afraid."

I was about to ask whether Holmes believed Cacy and his friends were involved, but our progress was suddenly halted by a young sergeant. He had come up alongside us on the road and was quite out of breath.

"Captain Watson, sir." The young man waited for me to return his salute. "Sir, I'm Sergeant Weaver. I work for Lieutenant Barthelme now, but I know you and this gentleman here are trying to come up with the bloke what killed Lieutenant Murtry. He was a good officer, sir. Treated the men right. It weren't right what happened."

He stopped to gulp some air and raced on. "I wanted to let you know what the lieutenant asked me to find out afore he was killed."

"Yes, Sergeant," said Holmes "We'd be very interested to know what you've discovered."

"Yes, sir." Weaver now addressed himself to Holmes. "It was like I told the lieutenant. Those Canadian blokes is missing two colt machine guns. They haven't reported it official like. They're trying to find them and not get laced into by the brass."

"Very interesting. Thank you, Sergeant. Should you find out any more, will you please let Dr Watson know? Your information may well help us find the lieutenant's murderer."

Sergeant Weaver was well pleased with Holmes' words and after a "You're welcome, sir" and a salute in my direction, he departed back toward the rail yard.

"My god, Holmes. We can't let those machine guns fall into the hands of the Boers. We must end this!"

"We will, old fellow, we will. The end is in sight."

"For you maybe. Where are you going?" Holmes had done an about turn and was headed back the way we had come.

"You, Watson, are going to the hospital. I am going to speak to a few people and find out where they were last night."

"Who?" I called.

"All the usual suspects!"

By now he was a hundred yards off.

CHAPTER 20

THE FOREIGN VOLUNTEERS

It was later than usual that afternoon when Cacy returned with the milk for the hospital. I had just walked outside when he arrived and called out for men to help unload.

"A horrible thing last night, doctor."

"That it was, Mr Cacy."

Cacy jumped down from the box as men pulled off the cans. Here was an opportunity for me to perhaps gain some information for Holmes.

"Did you see anything odd going on last night, Cacy?"

"Odd?"

"You know, man, unusual. Anyone there you hadn't seen before or someone perhaps arguing with Mrs Foster."

"Ah, no, I can't say as I did, Doctor. The boys and I left about ten as usual and went to Yagel's Hotel for a drink."

"Is anyone staying at the boarding house besides Major Drury?"

"Oh, yes, three or four officers. Mrs Foster's girl Molly could tell you who they are."

"What about Mrs Foster? Did she seem like she was upset or anything?"

"You've hit that right, Doctor. She was the shrew herself last night. I don't know what had happened, but she was all tears and meanness. Rest her soul." He crossed himself and looked to see if the cans were all off.

"I'm running late, doctor. Good day to you."

Cacy climbed back up in the box and called his mules to 'walk on'.

It was an hour or more later, near time to get something to eat, when Holmes finally re-appeared. He had spent the day verifying the location of everyone remotely involved in our drama. I suggested looking into the officers staying with Mrs Foster other than Drury.

"There are two lieutenants of artillery and a captain of engineers. All three were at their units late into the night. None returned before two this morning and their alibies are sound."

Holmes gave me a sly sideways glance and continued. "It seems that our friends Burnham and Fredericks were familiar with our late boarding house mistress also."

"Romantic or business?" I asked.

"Captain Burnham and his wife and child stayed with Mrs Foster in years back. He informed me of this when I told him of her death. He seemed to be truly saddened.

"Fredericks confessed he had met her numerous times when bringing hunting parties through. He also seemed to be genuinely upset by her demise."

"Holmes, this is too confusing. Everyone knows everyone. Half the people we know are involved with spying, and somewhere there is a person who does not mind solving all his problems with murder. How much worse can it get?"

"Never fear, Watson, we shall solve all. I see the clouds disappearing even now. You need a pipe and a meal, for we have a busy night before us."

"What are we to do?"

"I have left a message for your friend Mr Cacy. Unless I am very much mistaken, he will feel the need to tell some friends that Roberts will move tomorrow to re-take the water works. And when he goes, we shall follow him."

"You can't give away secret plans."

"Oh, Roberts isn't ready to move. If he were, Doyle would be dancing on your roof top. No, it is false information, but it should get the response we want."

"So Cacy is a spy." I sat on one of the benches fishing for my pipe in my pocket. "I must say I am disappointed. How long have you known?"

"Just about from the beginning," he replied, sitting with me. "Who better to move information than one who can move freely about the landscape? I suspect not only is he a loyal burgher, but a Fenian as well. Many are the Fenians who have been trained by the British army."

It was just getting dark when we arrived at the stables. I saddled Boy-O and Holmes had a Basuto pony he had borrowed. I felt ill-suited or ready for the task ahead. I neither knew the territory nor was I was much of a tracker. Hopefully Holmes was.

It was a short ride to a place down from which we could watch the barn behind the boarding house and not be seen. It was now nearly dark and I could see the lantern glow in the barn.

"Holmes, shouldn't we have someone with us? Like Burnham or Fredericks maybe? After all, this isn't like following a man through London. There won't be any cabs to catch or alleys to hide in or doorways for concealment. What was that?" I looked quickly around.

"Just a noise, Watson, just a noise. We shall do admirably, I'm sure. Ah, there they go. Quickly, Watson, to horse. We must not lose them in the darkness."

Cacy and the two other men had come out of the barn. Each led a horse and mounted once the barn door was closed. They walked their horses in the direction of Yagel's Hotel, but did not stop. We followed at a considerable distance. They slowly left the town. About a mile out they were stopped by the line of pickets. The pickets seemed well acquainted with the three horsemen and passed some banter before letting them go on their way. Of course, Cacy knew the day's password, so no suspicions were raised.

We followed once our quarry had moved on, gave the password and hurried into the darkness, trying not to lose the three men.

The moon was only at the half, but with no cloud cover the veldt was fairly lighted. We were able to keep the three men in view. As they would cross a small hill top, we would hurry to catch up, then drop to the military crest just below the skyline to search for the men. It seemed odd to me that they moved at a walk now that they had crossed the picket with valuable information such as they possessed. Why did they not rush pall mall for the Boer lines? Every hour would count if the Boers were to prepare a proper defence. I was soon to find out the reason.

They had just crossed a rather large Kopje and we hurried to catch up. As we crossed the hill top, we could see the three men in a donga not forty feet below. They had stopped their horses and sat with pistols pointed directly at us. I cursed our luck. "Holmes," I called, "run!" I started to turn Boy-O just as a man stepped from the darkness and grabbed his bridle. Another man had grabbed Holmes' horse and each held a Colt revolver.

"Now, boss. I wouldn't be trying to do nothin' dumb. You're caught and that's it." The man holding Boy-O's bridle grinned up at me. He wore a slouch hat, a waistcoat with brass buttons and canvas breeches. His face had the full beard of a Boer burgher, but the accent was definitely American.

"Off the horse now, Doctor, you too, Mr Holmes. Major MacBride will you be kind enough to bring Mr Holmes over here?"

Cacy, Seanan and Keenan had all ridden up to our little group. Cacy was shaking his head. "Doctor, it's sorry I am, but you've done this to yourself."

"Mr Cacy, how could you, a former soldier, become a traitor?"

"Sir, I'm no traitor. I'm a burgher. Sworn in at the start of the war we were. Besides, I enjoy fighting for the little guy. Be nice to him, Colonel, he's a good man." The last remark had been addressed to the man who had held Boy-O's bridle.

"Colonel Blake of the Boer Irish Brigade is it not?" asked Holmes.

"You've heard of me?"

"Yes, Colonel. Indian fighter, West Point graduate, now a soldier of fortune."

"No, Mr Holmes, there you are wrong. Just a little payback to England for what she's done to Ireland is all. Whenever we can, wherever we can." Cacy and his men chuckled at the remark.

"Tell me, Colonel, now that we are your prisoners, may I ask a few question of you and Mr Cacy?"

"I see no real harm. You'll be on your way to Pretoria before daylight as guests of the ZAR. What would you like to know?"

"Mr Cacy, is this where you came each night?"

"Yes. Mrs Foster always gave us some extra for the boys here. Food, whiskey, clothes and, as you've guessed, we brought information."

"Who was the source of the information you received?"

"Ah, now, that I don't know, sir. And wouldn't tell you if I did."

"Now is that all, Mr Holmes?" spoke up Blake. "We've much to do yet tonight."

"Just a couple more questions please." Holmes re-addressed Cacy. "I had, of course, noticed that the tracks made by your wagon were just as deep going out in the morning as coming back at night, which meant you were smuggling something. In addition, you actually had two wagons. One with Sarvin wheels, one with Archibald wheels. You switched them each day. Of course the wagon canvas with the painted harp was to keep everyone from looking too closely. What were you smuggling? "

"You are good Mr, Holmes. No use saying you're not. Yes, people see what they expect to see. The two wagons were similar, not identical, but with the harp painted on the canvas, well people just say, 'oh, that's Cacy coming' and don't look twice. It worked real well, it did."

"And the cargo?"

"False bottom, ya see. The McMullen boys here stole ammunition at the yard and put it in boxes of canned goods. The canned goods go in the ammunition boxes and get nailed back up. Some of these Tommy Atkins is going to be real surprised one day when they need some cartridges."

"The boys load the false bottom of the wagon at night. I take it out to that third farm we went to, doctor, and swap wagons so the boys can unload. And we do that every day."

"One last question," continued Holmes. "What about the stolen gold?"

"Mr Holmes, I swear I don't know anything about any stolen gold."

Colonel Blake held up his pistol hand.

"This is enough, Mr Holmes. It's time we were leaving. Keenan, bring up Fenian Boy and DG for the major and me."

Keenan was about to turn his horse in response to the Colonel's request when a voice sounded from behind me.

"Gentlemen, if you would be good enough to place your weapons on the ground." Churchill stepped out of the darkness with two men of the Mounted Yeomanry. In each hand he held a Mauser pistol with a 10 shot box magazine. The Yeoman had their Carbines pointed at the mounted men.

"Well, well. Mr Churchill isn't it? I've seen you in the papers I have." Cacy, Keenan and Seanan all still held their pistols in their right hands.

Complete silence reigned for a moment. Blake and MacBride had continued to hold their Colt single actions on myself and Holmes.

"It seems to me, boys, that what we have here is what we call in the States a 'Mexican standoff'! You can't shoot us 'cause we'll kill your boys here and you'll have a hell of a time explaining it. You may get us, but we'll get you. So how do you think we should work this?" Blake had pretty well summed it all up.

"I say," MacBride said breaking his silence, "that we all back off. Mr Cacy, you and the boys go on. Mr Churchill won't shoot. Will you Mr Churchill? That's a good lad."

Cacy and the boys backed their horses into the darkness until all we could see was a faint outline. "We're covering them, Major," called Cacy. "Come on."

Blake swept off his hat in an elaborate bow. Then he and MacBride backed into the donga where their horses were hidden. No sooner had they dropped from sight that Churchill started firing wildly pouring twenty rounds into the darkness. As the firing ended, I could hear Cacy's laugh. "I'm afraid you'll have to get another man to deliver the milk, Doctor. I'll leave word your to get it. Goodnight, Doctor." I heard their horses trot off.

"After them," cried Churchill to his men.

"No!" the order came from Holmes. "Who knows how many others there are out there? It is best we retire for now. But first I want to thank you, Lieutenant. Your help was indispensable as you saw."

The two men shook hands.

"I'm glad you let me in on it, Mr Holmes, though a couple of times I thought we'd lost you."

"You mean that Lieutenant Churchill was following us all the time?" I asked.

"Of course, Watson. That was the noise you heard earlier in town. I thought it advisable to have some extra protection, shall we say."

"Really, Holmes." I was quite agitated. "Someday you must learn to trust me." I mounted Boy-O in a huff and headed in the direction I believed I would find Bloemfontein.

CHAPTER 21

HOLMES PONDERS

Churchill and his men had reclaimed their horses in a moment and caught up with us.

"Sherlock Homes uncovers Boer Spy Ring," Churchill waved his arm across the sky. "'Report by special correspondent who aids great detective.' Yes, I can see the banner headline. If you gentlemen will excuse me, I must get to the telegraph office. I've a story to send."

Churchill put spurs to his horse. In a moment he and his two men were gone into the night.

"Alright, Holmes, we now know that Mrs Foster supplied information to Cacy, but where did she get the information? She has no real contact with headquarters or any of the men assigned there. And who killed her? Was it related or a lover's quarrel?"

"Watson, we have all but a few of the answers. Let us reason this out."

"Certainly, what do we know?"

"To start, we know that Cacy was moving information and ammunition to the burghers. For another, we know that Lieutenant Murtry was killed in Major

Parker's room. Why? He knew something he hadn't told us, but his enemy was aware of the discovery. Probably that Cacy had two wagons.

"Why was he in the room? To meet someone at the window or use the window as a method of egress.

"Who was free to move at night and meet him? Who also had access?"

"So you think Cacy….?"

"No, Cacy was out here on the veldt reporting. He most likely never even knew of the discovery."

"And Major Parker's murder?"

"Oh, the same reason, Watson. He discovered something or it was feared he was about to discover something. He trusted that knowledge to someone who he should not have. I believe he was following someone when he was killed. Someone who knew he was following."

"Alright, but why kill Mrs Foster? She was only a courier."

"Her death, as you said, could be related to the spy ring or personal, or both."

"And where did she get her information from?"

"I suspect that, of late, she had gotten all the information she needed from your friend Major Drury."

"Drury!" I exclaimed. "Never! He may be a lot of things Holmes, but I can't believe he's a traitor. He would never do such a thing."

"Oh, it is not intentional, Watson. It is an old story, though. Man wants to impress woman, woman feeds his ego and his whiskey glass. Man responds with a puffed up chest and tells her things he shouldn't to show how important he is - as I say, an old story."

"But where would Drury get any information? He's merely a liaison for a civilian hospital."

"Where does he spend his days, Watson?"

"At the headquarters." The wind now left my sail.

"And would anyone doubt his loyalty? Or, like you, would they take him to be the honest soldier he really is? They would have no reason to doubt him. His failing is not disloyalty, but drink and women."

We rode on in silence. It was just as we were coming to the pickets that I heard Holmes mutter, "Not the best of them, not the best of them" and shake his head. I know he was thinking about *'the woman'*, the one who had bested him, Irene Adler.

We gave the counter-sign and passed through the pickets before Holmes spoke again.

"I want to go back to the barn at Mrs Foster's, Watson. We haven't learned all of it's secrets yet."

"Secrets? What are you talking about? It's a barn."

"Oh no, Watson. Did you not ever wonder about the forge being used so constantly?"

"Well, yes but…"

"I believe I've just time for one pipe if we take our horses to the stables first. It is time to think, Watson."

In other words, he was saying, 'Watson, it is time to be quiet'. We rode on in silence.

Chapter 22

SECRET GOLD

By the time we had stabled the horses and walked back to Mrs Foster's barn, it was well past midnight. We opened the doors wide to let in what light there was. I was able to find a number of lanterns and lighted three or four.

"What are you looking for, Holmes? We have already been through here."

"I have missed something, Watson. I know I have. The keys are here, I must only find the lock." Holmes seemed to wander aimlessly around the interior of the barn. But I knew his movements were not aimless. There was great purpose. I seated myself on a keg and watched. Had I known what he was looking for, I would have helped.

Holmes went to the forge, now cold, and picked up various tools: hoof trimmers, pritchels, and tongs. He ran his hand around the inside of one of the iron pots and stared at his hand when he took it out. He put down the pot and started a tour around the exterior walls looking at boxes and bags and sheets of steel. Some sheets had holes, some not.

When Holmes came to the pile of canvas he reached into a wooden box and removed a set of grommet dies.

"Watson, do you notice something odd about these dies?"

I rose and went to his side, taking the dies from his hand.

"They seem to have been used quite a bit recently, Holmes. The surfaces are shiny, especially the head where you hit it with the hammer."

"Should there not be a stud on the upper half that centres the grommet while it is hammered firm on the canvas?"

I turned over the top die.

"Yes, Holmes. This die would be useless."

"No, not useless Watson. Hand me the bridle with the polished rosettes."

I went to the other side of the barn and returned with the requested item. Holmes immediately began to take the bridle apart. Removing the rosettes, he went over them carefully. Finally, placing one in his left hand, with his right he used the staple on the back and unscrewed the brass cover. Holmes smiled and lifted his right hand to show me that the brass decoration, when removed, revealed a steel stamp. The face of which showed the face of Paul Kruger. It was the size of a half-pond piece.

"Holmes, they were making money!"

"Yes, Watson, that is why you heard the ring of steel, but saw few shoed horses and no new wagon parts here." He pointed to the forge. "They would melt the gold in those pots, pour the molten gold into those iron sheets to rough the coins and then, while still hot, place the flans in the grommet dies, and using the stamps from these rosettes, make coin of the realm. The ringing you heard was a steel hammer hitting a steel die to impress the coin."

He smiled, almost to himself, and placed the rosettes in his pocket.

"Then Cacy lied about the gold."

"No, I don't think so. You asked him, Watson, about stolen gold. He did not consider it stolen."

"I guess there is that," I laughed. "And I suppose they carried the coins out in the wagon also. But why not leave it as bars?"

"Elementary! Coins are much, much easier to hide and distribute. Gold coins to be used for goods, services, and ammunition."

"So that is the end of it."

"No, Watson. They did not expect us tonight. We were poor at following our quarry. We should have done better. I don't believe Cacy saw us, but they were meeting Blake and either he or MacBride saw us and set the ambush. That means there should be more here. Had you noticed that the horseshoe kegs show no dust? Help me move them Watson."

In a moment, we had moved half a dozen quarter kegs of shoes and below was a trap door to what may have at one time been a root cellar. Each of us took a lantern. While I stayed above, Holmes descended a small ladder into the damp earth.

"Watson, I have something that may interest you," came Holmes' muffled voice. "Wait there." In an instant the barrel of a Colt machine gun appeared above the trap door. I grabbed it and placed the weapon on the forge. Holmes followed, coming up from the hole.

"Is the second one down there, Holmes?"

"No, Watson. I'm afraid that it is not. It, I fear, has already been delivered to our Boer friends. But there is something else."

"And that is?"

Holmes held out a gold bar. "I believe there to be about 5,000 ounces of gold down there. Surely something our friends won't want to leave. How maddening it must be for them. You recognize the weapon, of course."

I patted the side of the machine gun. "Yes Holmes, a Model 1895 Colt." It was then that Murtry's remark came back to me.

"Holmes, the potato digger!"

"Watson?"

"It was what Lieutenant Murtry was telling us. He said the plot involved two kinds of potato diggers."

For once Holmes looked at me blankly. It was a proud moment. I would be the fountain of knowledge.

"This Colt machine gun is called a 'potato digger'. It has an armature that comes out of the bottom of the receiver when it fires. If it is set too close to the ground, it digs furrows, hence the name." I took a breath. "The other type of potato digger was…"

"Yes, yes - Cacy and his men. A slur for an Irishmen. Well, you have cleared that up let us put the gun back and we shall be on our way."

"Put it back?"

"Of course. Otherwise they shall know we've found their secret hiding place. We do want them to come back. This game is not yet finished."

"No, Holmes, we can't take a chance on them getting away with this weapon."

"Watson, if you do not return the machine gun, it is probable that the real leak of information at the headquarters will find out. Once they know we have found the gold, they may decide to disappear. You must return it."

"Wait a moment. I thought you said Drury supplied the information to Mrs Foster."

"Of late, yes. But who supplied it to him? Who knew him well enough to know he would tell all to impress the woman?"

"I don't know." I was crestfallen.

"That, Watson, is what we've yet to find out. Now be good enough to give me the gun."

"In a moment."

It was much more than a moment before I gave the machine gun back to Holmes. He agreed to sit quietly while I struggled and strained and after many an error, finally determined how to remove the mechanism's firing pin. Then, with the light of false dawn, Holmes and I blew out the lanterns, replaced the kegs and departed.

CHAPTER 23

ONE LESS TRAITER

I did what I could at the hospital for the next few hours. By noon the lack of sleep had caught up with me and I went to a small copse of trees on the far side of the field. Here I rested and quickly fell asleep.

It was Moyer who found me what seemed like only moments later, but was actually three hours.

"I hated to wake you, Doctor, but Dr Doyle said to tell you that you and he are requested at the headquarters."

I rubbed my eyes and looked about. "What time is it?"

"Just four. Doyle says he'll wait for you at the pavilion."

I gathered myself together and walked with Moyer back to the hospital. Doyle was standing on the pavilion steps waiting.

"It seems we have been summoned to the headquarters where Holmes will 'reveal all', as they say in the detective novels."

"Yes, well, he'll have to wait a moment while I wash and get a clean shirt."

Grabbing one of the few dozen natives we employed, I pulled off my boots and gave the man instructions to give them a quick brush. In all, it was a delay of no more that fifteen minutes, but all the while Doyle was chewing his bit and anxious to go. One thing the army would never be able to teach the big man would be patience.

Having washed, put on a new shirt and pulled my boots back on, I re-joined Doyle and we walked toward the headquarters. I felt like I was being pulled along by a giant puppy on a leash, anxious to see the world.

We stopped at Barthelme's office and were taken on into Lord Roberts.

Roberts was sitting behind a large mahogany desk, looking rather sour of disposition. Disposed in chairs about the room were Churchill, Pelham, Burnham, Fredericks and Drury. Holmes stood by the French doors looking out into the tiny garden behind the hotel.

As we entered, Holmes greeted us. "Watson, Doyle, good. I thought it best we all be here."

"Can we begin now, man?" half-roared Roberts.

"Will Lord Kitchener not be joining us?" replied Holmes.

"No, now get to this; I've no time to dilly-dally."

179

Lieutenant Barthelme had entered with us, followed by an orderly carrying tea.

"Lord Kitchener is inspecting the Scots Brigade, Mr Holmes. He is not available." He turned to Roberts. "The tea, sir."

"Have him leave it on the table and get out. Not you Lieutenant, the corporal."

The corporal departed post haste and Barthelme tried to absorb himself into the wall by the door.

"Allow me, sir." Holmes poured tea and started handing it around, Lord Roberts first. Holmes was having too much fun. It showed on his face.

"I'll not say it again, begin, Mr Holmes. My time is precious." Roberts pushed his full tea cup away.

"Certainly, sir. Let me begin at the beginning, if I may. Of course you know all those present. Each has shared in our little investigation in some manner, so I felt they would want to be present. Some have had no part except to give aide. However, let me start at the beginning."

Holmes started by laying out the entire case at it had transpired. He spoke of his entire assignment from Mycroft, his stopping of the plot to damage the ports in Cape Town and his belief that both the gold and the information were reaching the Boers from this headquarters. Roberts snorted derision.

Holmes went on to explain our discovery of the system Cacy had used to move ammunition, gold and information provided by Mrs Foster to his compatriots in Blake's Irish Brigade. He finished by describing our search of the barn and his discovery of the dies and gold residue in the iron pots.

"And here, sir, are the dies that were being used." Holmes placed the two bridle rosettes on Roberts' desk. The general took up the two items presented and examined them. Then, placing them at the edge of the desk, he asked Holmes if he had found the gold also.

"Not yet, sir, it may have all been coined and moved. I do not yet know."

It was all I could do to sit still. Holmes must have his reason to lie to Roberts. I hoped all would turn out well. But that was only to be the first shock. I decided I could use some of that tea, but decided not to move.

"I understand, Mr Holmes." Roberts looked about the room a moment.

"Barthelme."

"Yes, sir.

"Go tell Mr Hatchett I want every ammunition box opened and checked."

"Yes sir."

Barthelme opened the door to go. As he went through, Roberts yelled after him.

"And don't tell him he's looking for canned vegetables!"

"No, sir."

"Now, Mr Holmes, let's get to the serious work. Who supplied Mrs Foster with the information she gave to this Cacy fellow?"

"Well, sir, it happened in two parts." Holmes walked about the room, moving from chair to chair, then back toward the French doors. He turned back to face the whole room. God he enjoyed being at the centre of the stage!

"The first part is rather sad, in a way. For Mrs Foster was a loyal Boer. She had lived almost her entire life in the Free State. She was widowed here and her children are buried here. So it was an easy task when our spy came to her and asked for her help.

"At first she was a bit hesitant. She was now surrounded by her enemy and she must learn to adapt. But her new friend quickly played on the woman's loneliness and became her lover. He had moved into the boarding house. So it was simple to bring information to her and let her pass it on to Cacy. It gave our man a degree of separation from the next level. Cacy only knew that Mrs Foster gave him information, not from whom it came."

Holmes paused as people started to look at Drury. After all, he lived there. Everyone knew he was sweet on the woman.

"I didn't!" Protested Drury in a state of anxiety.

Holmes went on. "We shall get to Major Drury in a moment." Holmes started walking about again as the door opened and Barthelme re-entered.

"No, in the first instance, our spy pre-dated Major Drury. I refer to Major Pelham."

"You're mad!" spit Pelham leaping from his chair. "Why would I pass information? What cause could I have? I've been loyal for twenty five-years. This is crazy."

"Oh, protest if you must, Major, but you promised the good woman marriage to make sure she co-operated. When I told Mrs Foster you were already married it all became clear. She was upset more than any casual acquaintance would be.

"You moved out of the boarding house when Major Drury arrived. You thought 'here is a man I can use'. He is sweet on Mrs Foster and he likes to bray. If I tell something to him, he will tell her when he drinks and I can separate myself even more'. In fact, you hoped that she would turn her affection to him and you could stop playing the lover."

"This is madness! Lord Roberts, surely you don't believe any of this," cried Pelham.

"Of course not. Holmes, this man has been with me for years, why since the Second Afghan War. You've no proof," stated Roberts.

Holmes stood nose to nose with Pelham. "Let me see your watch fob, Major."

Pelham didn't move. We were all now standing. Holmes reached forward and pulled the fob from Pelham's watch chain and without looking said, "Two headed coin of Ohm Paul," and threw it on the table.

Pelham stepped around Holmes. As he did so his pistol came out. Before anyone could react he had it pointed at Lord Roberts who had been the only one to remain seated.

"You, bastard! For twenty years I worked for you. Never a reward! Never a decent assignment! Who picked you up when you were injured at Kandahar? Who made sure you ate and drank and had paper to send out your snivelling little orders? I did! And now you wanted me to help kill my own people? I'll see you in hell!"

Pelham pushed the muzzle of the Webley into his own mouth and pulled the trigger. The room was soaked in blood and brains. Doyle ran to the body. I'd seen enough violent death; I felt no need to attend.

A moment later guards were flooding the room and Roberts was yelling at Barthelme. "Get it out of here! Now, Lieutenant."

Barthelme had the men carry the body out while two orderlies tried to soak up the blood with towels and wipe off the furniture. Roberts had re-seated himself after having jumped up at the gunshot. He pointed at Drury.

"I shall deal with you, sir. It's prison for you."

Drury was beside himself and protesting as best he could when Holmes intervened.

"Lord Roberts, you do not understand. While Major Drury was indeed passing information to Mrs Foster," -- Drury collapsed in a chair, head in hands, --"he was passing false information provided by me. He cooperated with me fully in rooting out this nest of spies."

I have never seen anyone more surprised than Drury was at that moment.

"The good, Major," continued Holmes, "agreed to my plan early on and has been of great benefit. This was the second part I spoke of." Holmes extended his hand to Drury. The major took it without rising and shook it limply. Drury was in as much shock as I was. "And now, Lord Roberts, I should like to stay a bit with my friend Dr Watson and shall trouble you no more. I will, of course, with your consent continue to look for the Boer gold, though I fear it may well be gone."

"Of course Mr Holmes. I have a good deal to thank you for." Roberts seemed a bit shaken. But his handshake was firm as, for some reason, he shook hands with all of us as we left the room.

"Well, so much for the spy ring Mr Holmes," grinned Churchill. "Well done, this will be quite a coup for me."

"What would that be?" asked Holmes.

"Why, a spy in the very centre of Lord Roberts' staff. 'Villain Takes Own Life'." He waved his arm in the air again.

"Why, whatever are you talking about, sir? Major Pelham died of enteric fever in Langman's Hospital. Isn't that so, Watson? Doyle?"

"Mr Holmes," laughed Churchill. "You can't hide this, it's too big. Everyone knows what happened."

"And what good does your story do, Lieutenant? Who does it help? Does it make anything better? Does it help at home or improve morale here?"

"But Holmes, you are a hero!"

"We are just doing what we can, Lieutenant. And there is more to do. We must find the 'Black Panther'."

"But I thought…"

"Oh no, Pelham was not the brains. He may have been a knight or bishop, but we must find the king. Good evening, Lieutenant."

Holmes, Doyle and I started our walk back to the cricket field.

"I don't know if you've stopped that story, Holmes," commented Doyle.

"Oh, I believe that if the story is written it might not be sent."

When we arrived at the pavilion, I stayed outside to talk to Holmes.

"What you did for Drury was a fine thing Holmes. He's not much, but he didn't mean harm."

"I know, Watson. This war has enough casualties. It does not need more."

I started laughing out loud. "The look on Drury's face when you bailed him out was priceless. I believe you have a friend for life."

"Perhaps, Watson. But sometimes doing a good deed breeds resentment. We shall see. And now I think it is time for a pipe."

Chapter 24

MEDICAL INSPECTION

On the morning of the 20th of April Holmes sent word to me that he was to have a private interview with Roberts in the morning. Come the afternoon, he would have need of me. To our good fortune, the hospital had received our additional volunteer. Dr Schwartz had arrived by the early up train and was hardly introduced when put to work.

Doyle was in a gleeful mood this morning, for word had come to us to assist in giving the mandatory medical inspection for the soldiers who would move against the water works. It would be good to see an end to the constant procession of dead. It seemed the dead march sounded constantly as soldiers moved down the roads with arms reversed.

Reveille had sounded at 5:30 as usual and by 6:15 five companies of yeomanry were in parade order in front of the tents outside the pavilion. I will admit it is a somewhat cursory inspection, but it is quite easy to identify those men who will have trouble on the march.

We had them remove boots and stockings and inspected each man's feet, hands, lungs, and ears and had a look in their eyes. This quick look would allow us to remove those that will fall out of the march early due to a defect. An army going to meet the enemy cannot afford the extra burden of men who are unfit, no matter how much those men want to help their mates.

By 9:15 the men were being marched off to the musketry range. There would be one more firing of all the weapons to check their serviceability. Once firing had been completed, each man would clean his weapon and then himself. It had always struck me as foolish to make the men use their mess tins to wash in, and then eat their meals from the same tin. But to have them carry even more equipment seemed just as bad.

Once the men had marched off to the musketry range, I returned to the pavilion and our rounds of the sick. Doyle decided to accompany the yeomen to the range. He was always appalled at the poor marksmanship of our men, especially when compared to the Boer foe.

Once back in England, both he and his friend, Kipling, would be driving forces in establishing shooting clubs throughout Great Britain. There would be over 1,000 clubs just before the Great War. It was a service neither he nor Kipling was ever properly thanked for. But that is a different story.

It was noon before I was able to take a break and sit with my pipe trying to collect my thoughts. Somewhere I must find another source of milk. I wondered if, without Cacy, the farmers would still sell to us. But Cacy had said that he would make it happen and for some reason I believed he would. It was then that I saw Drury for the first time that day.

"Captain, do you know where Mr Holmes might be? I would like to thank him. He saved my career yesterday. I have much to be grateful to him for."

For once Drury, appearing quiet and somewhat contrite, was sober and exuded no odour of alcohol. The shock of his actions and their possible consequences had evidently come home to him. It was one good thing that had happened so far.

"He was at the headquarters this morning, Major. I'm not really sure where he is now."

Drury sat on the bench next to me, his uniform clean and his boots shined in the sun. This man, I knew, would have to find additional work. Idleness would put him back where he had been, feeling his life and work had little purpose.

"Major, as you know, we have lost our man who was able to get us milk for the hospital. The milk makes a wondrous difference in the men and their recovery."

"Say no more, Watson, it shall be done. Do you know what farms were supplying the milk?"

"Well, yes. I've been there. I might draw a map for whoever goes."

"Good. You draw a map and I'll get a couple of men. I know that Mr Cacy's mules and wagon are still at the boarding house. If no one else has commandeered them for their own purposes, they will suit ours quite nicely. I'll be back."

Drury sprang from his seat. I could hear him calling names as he entered the pavilion. It was exactly what the man needed.

I had expected to see Holmes by now, but he was not to re-appear until much later in the day. In fact it, was while Doyle and I were taking some tea on the roof top that early evening when Holmes finally appeared.

"Welcome to the 'Café Enterique'," called Doyle as Holmes appeared on the stairs. "Would you care for some tea with your microbes?"

One had to forgive Doyle his odd sense of humour. Fatigue had set in. The long hours, the constant deaths, the dust and poor diet all made one a bit balmy.

"Most pleasant, Doctor. I could use some refreshment." Holmes seated himself on one of the boxes and accepted a tin cup from Doyle.

"How goes the search, Mr Holmes? Have you found your man?"

"I have devised a plan and I shall have it carried out tonight."

"What is our part?" Doyle said in a stage whisper leaning forward on his box.

"We - that is - the three of us, have no part in the plan except to wait."

"No!" cried Doyle. "We are not to be in on the kill?"

"What is your plan, Holmes?" I wanted to know as well and would also be disappointed not to be part of the final moment.

Holmes looked seriously at Doyle. "If I inform you, doctor, you must keep absolutely silent about all I say. Is that understood?"

"Yes, yes, of course."

"Well, I see no harm. Lord Roberts has agreed to it and given me a company of men." Holmes extended his cup and waited for Doyle to re-fill it.

"It is to be this way. Both Burnham and Fredericks have been given a mission tonight. Each has been briefed on an attack plan for the water works. But each has received a different plan. Neither is correct."

"Burnham and Fredericks?" interjected Doyle. "What have they to do with anything?"

"Who, Doctor, moves about constantly, is never noticed except in passing, and yet must be trusted with all the army's plans in order to properly do his job? Who did Pelham, Parker and Murtry have constant contact with? Who goes out into the night, unwatched, and unseen, to possibly not only spy on the Boers but contact them?"

"Well, then why weren't they doing that all along instead of using Cacy and his men?"

"For the simple reason that they weren't here. They are both fairly new arrivals."

"True." Doyle sat back and was pondering the fact.

"But surely not Burnham," I said. "He's loyal, a veteran of the Matabele Wars and all."

"He is also an American," responded Holmes. "Fighting natives might be one thing. Fighting what he may see as an independent nation like his own may be quite another."

"And Fredericks?"

"He is a Cape Boer. His family is now in the Free State somewhere. And you remember he was in Cape Town about the time I was dealing with Conway."

"You think he's Duquesne?"

"Either he or Burnham. How do we know Burnham was in Alaska? Right now we have only his word."

"Not a very trusting man, are you, Holmes?" Doyle was grinning from ear to ear. "So what is the rest of your plan?"

"As to that, each man goes on his scout tonight. Our friend, Churchill, has been detailed to take a couple of men and follow Burnham. I believe the easiest way to control our reporter is to keep him involved. He can put all this in his memoires when he's Prime Minister."

I laughed out loud at this.

"Oh, he will be, Watson, he will be. As to Fredericks, I've been given a Captain Saxon of Colonial Light Horse to follow him. Each man has the same instructions: follow, watch, report. We shall know if either man makes contact with the Boers to pass on the plan they have been given."

Holmes stayed a bit more and we finished our tea. Doyle and I finally gathered ourselves together to return below. I felt like I was descending into the bowels of hell. I think that when I die I shall stand before St Peter and behind him will be two gates - one marked Heaven, and the other, above the arch of the gate, will be the word "Bloemfontein".

Chapter 25

SCOUTING

It proved that the night's watch by Churchill and Saxon was futile. Neither Burnham nor Fredericks had made contact with anyone. Having completed their assigned tasks, both returned without incident to the headquarters. Holmes appeared upset that morning, but not completely disheartened. He had arrived as the men whom Major Drury had assembled for wagon duty were loading empty cans on what had been Cacy's wagon. It was the one with Sarvin wheels. I assumed his other was somewhere on the veldt. Drury had my map. Deciding it was safer to move in force, he had a half dozen extra mounted men with the wagon.

Today the soldiers who were destined to take Pretoria would be moving to staging areas for tomorrow's start toward the water works twenty miles distant. I watched as men of the Scots Brigade started loading kits, blankets and great coats into wagons. For now it looked like it was to be light marching order.

Light marching order meant that they might move more quickly, but they would also have no extra creature comfort. Sergeants were going down the lines checking each man. One blanket, 150 rounds of ammunition, water bottle (full of course), one day's ration in the haversack and a clean rifle. Off they marched to the East, pipes playing. I prayed they would all come out unharmed.

"What now, Holmes?" I asked as we watched the Gordons disappear down the dirt road.

"We continue the same plan as last night. Burnham and Fredericks will both be given scouts and Churchill and Saxon will follow."

"You're running out of time Holmes. Can't you just have Roberts arrest both men and hold them for now?"

"On what charge, Watson? I am convinced one of these two men is Duquesne. The problem is which? If we take out Duquesne we not only eliminate our current problem, but hopefully a future one.

"And what of the innocent man? Are we to destroy him for no other reason than to stop the first? Surely, the mere act of his arrest or detention would forever be remembered against him. No, Watson, we must be able to stop Duquesne without injury to others."

I handed Holmes a note I had received by messenger that morning.

"I'm thinking of doing this Holmes. After this I may be too old for active service."

Holmes read the letter which offered me a position on General Ian Hamilton's staff for the push to Pretoria.

"Well then, we must hurry and end our little puzzle so that you may join the advance. What does Doyle say of this?"

"Oh, he only wished it was he who had been offered the position."

"I understand that Rundle has already made contact with the enemy. There appears to be quite a bit of long range sniping, but Barthelme tells me they don't believe there are but about 3,000 Boers in the way."

"Only takes one to kill you," I said, taking out my pipe.

"Yes, remember, that old boy, I'd hate to lose you. When will you join Hamilton?"

"I've told them I'd be there on the 23rd. The day after tomorrow."

"Oh, we shall have finished by then, Watson."

I spent a few minutes that afternoon making sure my own kit was in order and arranging for a few boxes of medical supplies and equipment to be packed for me to take on the march. Most of the day was spent back in the pavilion and the tents full of sick men. I saw no more of Holmes that day, but he re-appeared just after midnight. I was unable to sleep and welcomed Holmes' company when he came to see me.

"I've asked Churchill and Saxon to report to me here if you do not mind, Watson. I knew you would want to be in on things at the last."

"I appreciate the company Holmes. Have a seat. Sorry I've no brandy to entertain with. You'll have to settle for a pipe."

"Exactly what I should like, my friend."

Holmes and I sat in silence for the better part of an hour before we were interrupted by the sound of horses below. This was followed by the sound of foot-falls on the steps. Holmes continued to sit and smoke while I rose to see who our visitors might be.

Churchill and Saxon followed each other onto the roof.

"Good evening, Doctor, Mr Holmes." It was Churchill who spoke first. "I'm afraid we both have bad news for you Mr Holmes." He threw himself down on a box.

"Neither man made contact with anyone that we could see." He looked to Saxon, who shook his head in confirmation. "You may be on a completely wrong trail here, sir."

"There was nothing either man did?" Drop something perhaps, or mark a rock or tree?"

Both men shook their heads again, but then Saxon looked thoughtful for a moment.

"What is it, Saxon?" pressed Holmes. "The smallest thing may be of the greatest importance."

"Well, sir - It probably means nothing at all, but, well, both tonight and last night Fredericks got down and checked his horse's right front hoof. Like he was checking for a stone or maybe he felt the animal was going lame. I never saw the horse limp, but sometimes you can feel it, you know, that the animal is stepping just a little lightly on one foot."

Holmes stood up and went over to where Saxon stood.

"Now think carefully, man. Where did he do this? Was it at the same place each time?"

"Now that you mention it, Mr Holmes, it was. I remember thinking it odd at the time that the animal should go lame at the same spot."

Holmes clapped the Captain on the back. "Excellent, my good man, excellent. We shall have him."

"Then Fredericks is our spy!" I exclaimed.

"Perhaps, Watson."

"But you just said..."

"Watson, Watson. Can you charge a man with spying or treason for checking a hoof?"

"But you believe it is he, don't you, Mr Holmes?" said Churchill.

"Yes, I believe he spotted Captain Saxon here and used that method to warn off his contact. Tomorrow he shall not be followed."

"Captain, can you find that same spot in the daylight?"

"Yes, sir, I'm sure of it. That will not be a problem."

"Good. I will need you and about twenty men. Oh, yes you may come along also, Mr Churchill. Meet me here at about seven tomorrow night." He looked at his watch, it was now past 2 am "Or maybe I should say tonight. And now Watson, I will leave you. I have much to coordinate. Goodnight."

Saxon and Churchill said their good nights also. I was left to finish my pipe and get what sleep I could.

Chapter 26

THE AMBUSH

It was only two hours later that I heard, at 4 a.m., reveille sounding throughout the town. I was anxious to go but would wait this one more day for Holmes.

I rolled back over on my cot, but sleep was not to come. The noise from below kept me from sleep. Most of the army was already eight or ten miles to the north or east of Bloemfontein in their assembly areas. Those moving now were support elements and their escorts.

I finally decided to get up and light a pipe. Below, lines of wagons stretched as far as the eye could see in both directions. Wagons pulled by ten span of oxen and guided by natives with huge whips, mule wagons, and horse drawn wagons, wagons filled with the supplies of war.

Their escorts of marching men and mounted infantry walked or rode to each side and opened their distance to the flanks for protection as the line of supply disgorged itself from the town, giving the appearance of a huge inverted funnel.

There was the creaking harness, the rumble of wheels, the sound of drivers yelling at their teams. If I closed my eyes I was back in Afghanistan. How little things had changed.

Having finished my pipe, I went below to start my rounds in the pavilion. I had a biscuit and some tea at some point in the morning, but it was Holmes' arrival at about noon that finally caused me to take a break.

We went to our mess area and, taking a cup of tea went out under one of the trees which covered some benches.

"Holmes, I've been meaning to ask, has anything happened at Mrs Foster's barn? Anyone come to get the gold?"

"No, Watson, though I've had the barn watched constantly. It is a little hard to accept that they would make no attempt to recover such a sum."

"They'll have to reclaim the gold soon or give it up for lost. If what Rundle reports is correct, they will be pushed beyond reach of it in short order."

"Or, perhaps, they are content to leave it there and decide what to do about it when their cause is lost."

"You mean, keep it for themselves?"

"Let us say, as an insurance policy. If Fredericks is in fact Duquesne as we believe, he may decide he needs a certain amount of treasure to escape. No, Watson, I do not believe that we are watching that cache in vain. If nothing happens by the time we leave here tonight, Barthelme has orders to remove the gold and return the machine gun to the Canadians." Holmes finished his tea. "It was not a sure thing anyway."

Our conversation was now interrupted by a detachment from General Hamilton's staff. They had been ordered to collect my kit and I took leave of Holmes, who promised to return by seven. I spent the afternoon working with Dr Schwartz and thanking the many members of Langman's Hospital with whom I had become so familiar. It was especially hard to part with Moyer, Gibbs and Scharlieb. There would be time later that night to say adieu to Langman and Doyle, who had made the decision to accompany the troops on the assault of the water works. Doyle desperately wanted in on the fighting. Langman, however, was more curious than wanting to fight. Both, I knew, would find Pole-Carew's staff to see the fight. They would be off before sundown to catch up.

By five o'clock I was over at the stable where I found Boy-O almost alone. There were but half a dozen horses left in this one area, all of which belonged to members of Lord Robert's staff.

Having groomed and saddled my fine bay, I walked him back to the hospital and checked my equipment one more time. I was one who believed that British cavalry and mounted troops were overloaded with equipment. But my thoughts, though I'm sure shared by others, I kept to myself. Since I was to be on staff, I could do certain things which a soldier could not. I had stripped down all my equipment to the barest few things. I carried my Webley-Pryse pistol and left the sabre. My saddle bags carried but ammunition, a metal mirror for signalling, a day's rations, and spare horseshoes. My great coat was packed on the saddle along with oats for Boy-O. Besides my revolver I wore my double brace Sam Browne belt, water bottle and haversack. I had discarded my helmet for a slouch hat which I turned up on the left side. I had taken special care to double blanket Boy-O. I had learned to do that on campaign in Afghanistan. It was easier on the animal and I was always able to swap the blankets, keeping a dry one near his back. It helped to prevent galling. My haversack was filled with medical supplies. On the saddle's near side, where normally hung the sabre, was a second haversack with additional bandages and medications. The pommel bags held only cigars, matches, and a pint of brandy. A small set of binoculars hung from my neck.

It was now near seven and I had not long to wait until Holmes came up on his Basuto pony. We had but said hello when the rest of our party gathered. There was still a good hour and an half of daylight to be had, but Holmes wasted no time. As soon as Captain Saxon arrived with his twenty men, we started toward the Veldt. Saxon and Holmes were in the lead. Behind them came myself and Churchill, followed by Saxon's men. We moved in silence as we passed first supply, then infantry and cavalry units bivouacked for the night. From ahead came the roar of artillery. Pole-Carew was trying to weaken the Boer defences before tomorrow's battle. After a fast-paced ninety minutes, we passed some of the artillery on our left. Twilight was upon us. The flashes of the muzzles lit the sky and gave the gunners an unreal appearance as they moved calmly about their duties, their blue leather gaiters reflecting the muzzle flash of the cannons.

Now we were ahead of the guns and moved down into a donga which ran to the northwest and below the trajectory of the artillery firing over our heads. We finally stopped near a saddle between two Kopjes and dismounted. Horse holders took our mounts back around into a deep part of the donga as the rest of us made our way up the west side of the saddle. About half way to the top, Saxon split his men. Half he placed in extended order along the south side, the other half on the west, setting up an L-shaped ambush. Many are the men who have been killed by their own comrades in a cross fire. This would not happen here.

Holmes, Churchill, Saxon and I placed ourselves in the angle of the L and settled down to wait. As darkness completed its' shroud the artillery fire started to die off. Until, unable to see their target any longer, the cannons fell silent. The Boers knew we were coming. The only question was where would be the main attack. Fredericks believed he knew the answer to that question.

Hour upon hour we waited. The occasional cough or sneeze of a soldier down the line sounded like an explosion in the stillness of the night.

"Are you sure we are in the right place?" whispered Churchill to Saxon.

"Yes, this is it. He'll be along."

"It's almost midnight already."

Holmes held up his hand. "Quiet" was the inaudible command. I tensed. The last three hours had been excruciating. No talking or movement, no smoking for fear that the glow or the smell would give us away. My bones ached, but if I moved the creak of my leather seemed to have the loudness of church bells.

Holmes pointed silently to the right. Entering our trap was a man on horseback. He moved slowly and searched all about him as he rode. Surely, I thought, he must see the men to my right. He looked to be almost upon them. But it is true that, at least in the night, it is difficult to see an object plainly, unless it moves. Our attention is always drawn to an object in motion. Something that does not move is easily overlooked.

On rode our quarry. I could see him plainly now. I could not make out his face, but by the hat, and his movements, it was Fredericks. He rode to a place not more than twenty yards from us and stopped his horse. Taking a final look around at the rocks and boulders which surrounded him, he stepped out of the saddle and raised his mount's left front hoof. I looked to Holmes who smiled, acknowledging my thought. The left hoof meant all was clear.

Suddenly, like apparitions from a ghostly world, half a dozen men appeared out of the darkness.

"What news, Fitz?" said the man in the lead.

"You know the attack is at first light," responded Fredericks.

A couple of the men laughed. One spoke to another, but I did not understand Dutch and so did not know what was said.

"Yes, Paul. The cannons were a clue. But they won't attack from there." Fredericks had knelt in the dust and was drawing a map in the dirt with a stick. "They come from here, from the south-east. They think the guns will make you move your men to the north-west, but Rundle is there and will hold you in place while they roll up a flank that they hope is lightly held."

"It is a good plan," said the Boer. "I'm not sure if we have enough men to hold in any case. I will report this to the general. Will you come away with us?"

"No, Hans. I go back. As far as I know you are moving all your men from this area. That's what I'll report. I'll report where and when I can. Back here tomorrow if you hold."

"As I said," replied Hans, "that is for the generals. God go with you."

The two men shook hands and Hans turned to go.

Fredericks pointed at the man whom he had called Paul. "And keep Paul out of trouble and away from the women!" The group laughed and disappeared into the darkness.

I looked to Holmes. Churchill and Saxon did the same. Were we to let them get away? What were we doing out here if not to capture Fredericks and his men.

The adrenalin was pouring through my veins. We must move before he got away.

Holmes just smiled at us and stood up. Duquesne, as I shall call him now, had watched his Boer companions leave and had not yet mounted. We were on him in an instant, before he could draw a weapon or put a foot in a stirrup. Saxon reached in Duquesne's holster and retrieved the spy's pistol.

"Well played, Mr Holmes, well played." Duquesne was smiling in spite of his plight. He looked into the darkness where his comrades had disappeared.

"Oh, they are within earshot, sir. But their duty is to get the information you gave them back to their general. They will not be back." Holmes was, of course, correct.

"We must stop them! They have important information." Churchill had both of his pistols out and was frantic.

"No need, sir. The information was quite incorrect. Rundle will hold, but the attack from the southeast is but a feint and the main attack is where it should be, under the protection of the guns. Let them go."

"It might be best if we chased them a bit, Mr Holmes." Saxon had spoken up for the first time. "They may think it odd if we did not."

"Excellent point, Captain. But please, do not catch them. Watson, Churchill and I will await your return with Mr Duquesne."

"That's, Captain Duquesne," stated our prisoner.

In a moment horse holders had been called up, the men mounted and with much noise and to-do "gave chase" to the Boers. Churchill seemed quite put out, and taking his horse, which had been brought up with ours, he walked to a distant rock to pout.

"You didn't let him go on purpose, Holmes."

"Something about that man irritates me, Watson. I'm afraid he will make his way stirringly in the government. It will do him good to have to wait for things now and then. Ah, but Captain Duquesne, we are neglecting you."

While Holmes was busy talking, I had taken to watching Duquesne. One man who had been left with us was tying our guest's hands behind his back. He'd be able to ride, but his horse would be led.

"While we are waiting for our friends to return, would you mind answering a few questions, Mr Duquesne?" asked Holmes.

"Not at all, Mr Holmes, although I think you probably know all there is to know, with one exception."

The man looked about then seated himself on a large rock. Churchill came back to where we stood.

"If you are wondering why I did this, the reason is simplicity itself. I hate you bastards." Duquesne smiled as he said the last sentence, not angrily, but in a voice as calm as if he had been sitting at the dinner table.

"You push my people off their land and when they move and re-establish themselves, you decide you want that, too. You murder and plunder and steal and then you ask why we fight you. You're well aware it is about the gold and the diamonds."

"You abuse our citizens," interjected Churchill.

"They were treated well. Why would we give them the vote? They were not citizens! You may tell lies to yourself, but the world knows what this is about."

"If I may interrupt your political discussion," said Holmes. "You ran the sabotage organization at the port in Cape Town?"

"Yes."

"And you had men in place to move the stolen gold. They were yours, of course."

"There was stolen gold. Stolen from the Boer people and retaken by them."

"Of course," Holmes bowed, "and Pelham was the reason you came to Lord Roberts' headquarters."

"Yes, he was weakening. He could see things were starting to go against us. So he was becoming afraid of his position. Maybe he would have to give his whole thing up. Like most British, he needed to have his back stiffened."

"And yet we win, don't we," snarled Churchill. "The Empire not only stands, it grows."

"For now, perhaps."

"Enough," said Holmes. "I've no time for this. Is there anything else you would care to tell us, Captain Duquesne?"

"Just one thing, Mr Holmes. Don't expect to find any gold when you get back to Mrs Foster's."

"It'll be there," I said. "It's being watched."

"Yes, Doctor, by my men. Well, they're technically MacBride's men. They relieved your guard mount just after dark. Fine looking lot of Royal Irish they were. The gold, machine gun and ammunition were loaded and are now within the Boer lines." A smile ran across the scoundrel's face from ear to ear.

"As you said earlier, sir. Well played. Well played" replied Holmes. "Mr Cacy, I suppose?"

"Yes, he and the McMullen boys."

"And the uniforms were taken from the Irish Rifles who surrendered last month."

"Yes, again, Mr Holmes."

"And the deaths of Lieutenant Murtry, Major Parker and Mrs Foster?"

"Hated to do Murtry, he was a nice lad. Wanted me to take him to watch Cacy, I couldn't allow that. Parker I sent out to be taken care of by the boys. Told him where to find Cacy, poor man didn't know when to surrender. As to Mrs Foster," he thought for a moment. "Never rely on a woman Mr Holmes, they are too emotional." Holmes glanced at me with a smirk. "She," continued Fredericks, "would have given us up for spite just to get at Major Pelham. I had to remove her."

Saxon and his men had now returned. The private who had remained with us helped Duquesne up on his horse and passed the bridle reins to another man.

"I'll take those reins," said Churchill. "I owe a Boer a ride into captivity."

Looking to his captain, who nodded, the man passed the reins to Churchill who led off without waiting for the rest of us. I was tempted to depart from my friend here and try to find Pole-Carew and his men, but I realized I would be far better off returning to Bloemfontein and getting the best location they could give me and a few hours of sleep.

Holmes and I stopped at Mrs Foster's barn to find the cellar empty except for a lone coin which had been laid on the top of the trap door. It was a coin with two heads.

Chapter 27

THE WATER WORKS

"I'm sorry, Holmes. You couldn't have known that they would come back in uniform." I felt sorry for my friend's failure. Even though he had captured the spy, Duquesne, any part of his plan going astray always bothered him.

"Watson, do you really think I would leave the gold here when just such an eventuality was possible? I'm afraid the boys will find that they not only have a non-functioning 'potato digger', but also a number of boxes of horseshoes instead of gold." Holmes flipped the coin over to me. "A souvenir for your collection, Watson. You may put it in the box with your ruby.[3]

"I also gave a note to the boys' sister Molly. She was to give it to Cacy if she saw them loading the wagon."

---

[3] See *Watson's Afghan Adventure,* MX Publishing

"What did the note say?"

"Well done!"

Holmes and I rode on to the headquarters. The sun was rising and I needed to rest and feed Boy-O. He would be no good if he were over worked. The morning's battle would have to wait.

Lieutenant Barthelme greeted us as we arrived with word that Roberts was in an exceptionally good mood. It was expected that the day's battle would go well. Burnham had returned before dawn with critical information. The Boers had been drawn to exactly where he wanted them. Their centre had been weakened when they sent re-enforcements to the south-east. Now Roberts' forces would attack the weakened centre under the protection of the guns.

"Then everything has gone as planned." Churchill had entered the room. "I will wait until the end of the day and wire the good news to the world. But first I must write up last night's adventure."

"Where is your charge, Mr Churchill?" Holmes looked concerned.

"In Major Parker's old office, I put a man on the door. Not to worry. He'll be off on the next train to prison in Cape Town."

"I think I have one more thing I would like to discuss with Captain Duquesne. If you gentlemen will excuse me." Holmes went off down the hall.

I agreed to some tea offered by Barthelme. Churchill sat at an empty table with notebook and pencil scribbling furiously.

"Have you seen Lieutenant Langman and Doctor Doyle, Captain?" I was curious if they had gone out to the Water Works.

"Yes, Doctor, they left early last evening. I imagine they slept under some wagon or other. They wanted to be in on the battle."

"Well, I think we are done here, Watson." Holmes had returned and stood in the doorway. "Shall we take care of the horses? Then I know you want some sleep and I must arrange to go to Cape Town. And Lieutenant Churchill, I should like to ask a question. Did you leave the Captain alone in Major Parker's office?"

Churchill had a startled look. "Yes, why? Is he not alone now?"

"He is not there now, my good fellow. You really should not leave a prisoner alone. You, of all men, should know that."

Except for Holmes, we pushed from the room. Parker's office had been on the first floor. We raced up

219

the stairs, past the guard, and through the door. The room was empty and the window was open.

"He's gone," yelled Churchill. "After him."

I grabbed the fellow by the sleeve as he tried to rush past. "After him, where? By now he probably has a half-hour start. And which way did he go? East? I wouldn't. I'd go North or West. You've lost him old boy, calm down."

Churchill ripped himself free and ran down the stairs and out the front door, Barthelme was in close pursuit.

I descended and met Holmes in the hallway.

"Watson, I don't think we shall read of this adventure in the papers." It was as close to a laugh as I'd seen on Holmes in quite a while.

"Now you have to start all over, Holmes."

"No, Watson. Duquesne may be back, but for now his spy ring is broken and at least we have recovered some of the gold. I think it is time for me to return to Baker Street. Let us put up the horses and have some refreshment."

Come the afternoon I took leave of Holmes to go in search of Langman and Doyle, with a promise to return the next day to bid farewell. Holmes had agreed to stay one additional day to give some recommendations to Parker's replacement, who was to arrive that evening.

On finding Doyle, near the Modder, he was all news and excitement. He and Langman had indeed slept under some wagons and seen Hamilton consolidate his forces for his day's battle - a battle that Doyle thought "magnificent".

"I admit, Watson, I was a bit concerned when we came through Sanna's Post, where we had that disaster a few weeks ago. Dead artillery horses lying about everywhere, the place covered with the litter of war – puttees, broken helmets, haversacks, belts. It was depressing. But you should have seen the men this morning."

"Quite the show, eh?"

"Hamilton was already there, of course, but Smith-Dorrien brought up his brigade this morning. Straight up the middle, extended order, and when the Boers moved men from their left to help the centre, our mounted infantry swept round and rolled them up."

"And the casualties?" I asked.

"Oh, very light, considering."

I was a little put out by Doyle. I know I should not have been, but while the war was being fought, I could not think of casualties without sadness.

"Going to move with the army or is the hospital staying here?" I asked.

"We'll be moving when Roberts does," replied Langman. "Probably in a week or so, in the meantime we shall finally get clean water."

"Yes, you know the battle may be "magnificent" as you say, Doyle, but to the soldier it is a minor thing. To him it's the need for clean water, firewood, enough biscuits for the march and how to get away with a chicken and not get punished. It's trying to stay dry or cool or warm and keeping his feet from blisters. Those are the real important things in life."

"You cannot bring me down, Watson; they did a glorious job today. But tell me, what of you and Holmes? Has he solved his mystery?"

I explained the events of the last few days to my two companions as we rode back toward Bloemfontein and the Langman Hospital. It was almost a four-hour ride and pitch black by the time we got there. The rest of the staff was overjoyed with the news that fresh water would soon be flowing again.

I left Doyle regaling the crowd with tales of the great battle, gave Boy-O to a groom and lay out on my old cot on the roof. I was asleep in an instant.

DENOUEMENT

The next day I tarried a bit longer than I should have. I was already a day late reporting in to Hamilton's headquarters, but I felt my reasons would be acceptable. I took my leave of the staff at Langman's. Finding Holmes, I went with him to the railroad station to see him off.

"You've done well, Holmes. You've succeeded in everything that Mycroft asked of you."

"True, Watson. It is unfortunate that Lestrade let Duquesne escape."

"Churchill, you mean."

"Yes, Churchill, just a slip of the tongue. We shall see more of both of them I'm afraid. How soon will you return?"

"If Lord Roberts is to be believed we'll be done in three months. He's going to push straight to Pretoria. But I don't know, I'm not sure just taking the South African capital will end it. They may fight on."

"Take care of yourself, old boy. I shall tell Mrs Hudson to expect you in August."

I had to laugh at this precise prediction and we shook hands as he entered the train. I stayed on the platform until the train had disappeared from sight. Having mounted Boy-O, I started a long ride to catch up with Hamilton.

On the 5th of June we marched into Pretoria. Roberts would consider his work done, having annexed the two Boer Republics as new British Colonies. Before the end of July he and I were on our way home to England.

I saw Langman and Doyle occasionally and by mid-July Doyle, was also on the way home wanting to be the first to turn out a precise history of the Boer War.

Churchill returned about the same time with his usual criticisms of whatever was done.

Kitchener took over from Lord Roberts and became involved in a terrible guerrilla war that lasted two years.

As for Duquesne, he escaped to England, joined the British army and received a commission as a lieutenant and returned to Cape Town. He states that his sister was murdered and his family farm burned by Kitchener's army. His mother was raped and she and the baby died in one of Kitchener's concentration camps. Duquesne used his new position in Cape Town to organize another ring of saboteurs, who were only caught because one man did not want his own property destroyed. Of the twenty men who were captured, only Duquesne was not executed, upon his giving to the army the secret to a Boer code. He was sent to prison in Bermuda, from where he escaped. In the Great War he would spy for the Germans, sink British ships with bombs and claimed to direct the submarine that killed Lord Kitchener. He had his revenge.

I saw a good bit of work accomplished by MacBride, Cacy and the McMullen brothers. They had become the 'wrecking crew' of the Boer army. Not a bridge was taken on the way to Pretoria. The Irish Brigade's men, always the final guard, blew them apart.

Burnham was wounded in early June but had accomplished incredible things. I hope he someday writes his memoires. He was offered the Victoria Cross, but refused as it would have required the giving up of his American citizenship. He and Churchill returned to England aboard the same ship.

Boy-O I hated to part with. He served me well and was a good companion on the veldt. I left him in the care of Lieutenant Barthelme and the last I knew Boy-O was serving out his retirement on pasture near Cork City.

As for myself, I have had the second, no third, adventure of a lifetime. The first two being: Afghanistan and the friendship of Sherlock Holmes.

As Holmes had predicted, I was back in Baker Street in August, just in time to assist in the story I have decided to call "The Adventure of the Six Napoleons".

Also From MX Publishing

Winners of the 2011 Howlett Literary Award (Sherlock Holmes book of the year) for '**The Norwood Author**'

From one of the world's largest Sherlock Holmes publishers dozens of new novels from the top Holmes authors.

www.mxpublishing.com

New in 2012 [Novels unless stated]:

Sherlock Holmes and the Plague of Dracula
Sherlock Holmes and The Adventure of The Jacobite Rose
[Play]
Sherlock Holmes and The Whitechapel Vampire
Holmes Sweet Holmes
The Detective and The Woman: A Novel of Sherlock
Holmes
Sherlock Holmes Tales From The Stranger's Room
The Sherlock Holmes Who's Who [Reference]
Sherlock Holmes and The Dead Boer at Scotney Castle
The Secret Journal of Dr Watson
A Professor Reflects on Sherlock Holmes [Essay
Collection]
Sherlock Holmes of The Lyme Regis Legacy
Sherlock Holmes and The Discarded Cigarette [Short
Novel]
Sherlock Holmes On The Air [Radio Plays]
Sherlock Holmes and The Murder at Lodore Falls
Untold Adventure of Sherlock Holmes
Sherlock Holmes and The Terrible Secret
Sherlock Holmes and The Element of Surprise
Sherlock Holmes and The Edinburgh Haunting
The Hound of The Baskervilles [Play]
56 Sherlock Holmes Stories in 56 Days [Reviews]
The Many Watsons [Reviews]
The 1895 Murder

Also from MX Publishing

Sherlock Holmes Travel Guides

London   Devon

In ebook (stunning on the iPad) an interactive guide to London

400 locations linked to Google Street View.

Also from MX Publishing

Cross over fiction featuring great villans from history

 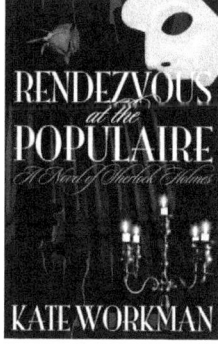 

Fantasy Sherlock Holmes

Links

Save Undershaw   www.saveundershaw.com

Sherlockology   www.sherlockology.com

MX Publishing   www.mxpublishing.com

You can read more about Sir Arthur Conan Doyle and Undershaw in Alistair Duncan's book (share of royalties to the Undershaw Preservation Trust) – An Entirely New Country and in the amazing compilation Sherlock's Home – The Empty House (all royalties to the Trust).

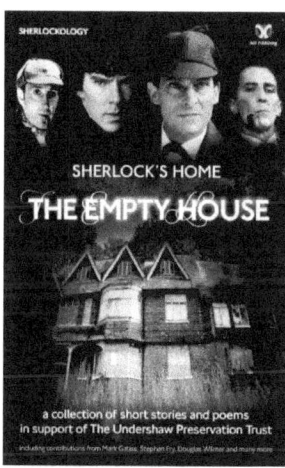

www.ingramcontent.com/pod-product-compliance
Lightning Source LLC
Chambersburg PA
CBHW071144260626
47162CB00003B/907